A MURDER WITHOUT MOTIVE

LISETTE DARLING GOLDEN AGE MYSTERIES

LISETTE DARLING GOLDEN AGE MYSTERIES
BOOK 3

COLETTE CLARK

DESCRIPTION

Not a case of whodunit...but *why*dunit?

Hollywood 1935

Lisette Darling doesn't know why she's been invited to Franklin Winthorpe's yacht for the birthday celebration of his latest love interest, Verity Vance. But with a guest list that includes a nice slice of Hollywood royalty, she's happy to hop aboard for a weekend trip along the Pacific Coast.

At least until a shot rings out, and one of the guests is murdered.

Verity is the one holding the smoking gun and doesn't deny shooting it.

The only question is...why?

Lisette is perfectly fine leaving it to the police to figure out the motive. That is until Franklin begins using his influence to suggest those on board didn't see what they think they saw, and the actual shooter may have been Verity's doppelgänger...Lisette Darling.

***A Murder Without Motive* is the third book in the *Lisette Darling Golden Age Mysteries* series**

set in 1930s Hollywood. Take a trip along the Pacific Coast aboard a yacht in this twisty, cozy mystery amid the glitz and glamour reminiscent of classic films.

CHAPTER ONE

THE LOS ANGELES POST

Murder or Tragic Accident on Winthorpe Yacht?
Hedley Harper

July 17, 1935

IN HOLLYWOOD, fiction is occasionally used to wildly embellish the truth. This is sadly the case with the rumors regarding the death of a certain individual aboard a certain yacht this past weekend.

Yes, there was a tragic death. However, the stories surrounding the unfortunate event have ranged from inaccurate to outright delusional, considering the outlandish leaps made and liberties taken with regard to the facts of the matter. This reporter won't name names, but a certain scribbler who *claims* to accurately depict stardom today should learn to be more judicious with both the paintbrush she uses to artfully color the truth in her stories and the source of her paint.

As someone who was aboard the yacht at the time, it behooves me to set the record straight. After all, what better resource for the unvarnished truth than someone with a firsthand account of the events? For the sake of justice, it is my duty to lend a note of honesty and gravitas to the death, which has been garishly bandied about by loose lips in the most tawdry manner. All when there hasn't even been a name attached to the *supposed* victim of murder.

Out of concern for the family of the deceased, and by order of the authorities, I too shall refrain from naming the individual who tragically passed this weekend. I can, however, attest to the fact that, from what I witnessed, the death seemed to be a terrible accident, nothing more.

Yes, the young and lovely Verity Vance has been taken into custody and charged with first-degree murder. However, rest assured, dear reader, the facts of the case will unfold over the next few weeks. They will shed light on her supposed guilt and rehabilitate her good name and immaculate reputation, as well as that of the very successful Franklin Winthorpe.

As of now, one glaring fact cannot be ignored, the police have nothing that even approaches the level of motive for murder. In fact, Miss Vance was a most gracious hostess to all, charming even the most recalcitrant guest. If you'll indulge a bit of subjective editorialization, I confess that Verity is the last person out of all those aboard I'd believe capable of murder. I firmly believe she will be found innocent of all charges.

The not-so-subtle digs at her Hollywood tabloid competition aside (Lorlene Divine, who authored the column "Hollywood Lives" in Rutherford Heart's *American Herald,* was probably already scribbling her response), Hedley had made a decent attempt to whitewash Verity Vance's reputation in preparation for her trial. It wouldn't be long before the Winthorpe Media propaganda machine went to work trying to sanitize the "death" even more in the coming weeks.

Hedley and every reporter who worked for the Winthorpe Media empire could proclaim Verity's innocence until the ink ran dry in their presses. However, those who were aboard Franklin Winthorpe's yacht that weekend knew the truth: Verity Vance had been the one holding the gun.

Still, Hedley had managed to stir an ounce of truth into her sycophantic gloss: not a single person aboard the *Veni Vidi Vici* could fathom Verity's motive for murder.

CHAPTER TWO

IT WAS impossible to miss the Winthorpe yacht docked in Marina Del Rey, as it was the biggest one there. As if Franklin Winthorpe would have had it any other way. He not only represented the West Coast interests of the Winthorpe Media empire, he personified it. Everything he did was bigger, better, and glitzier than anyone he saw as a competitor, including his older brother in New York, Edgar Winthorpe, who was the real head of the business.

That no doubt explained the name of Franklin's yacht, *Veni Vidi Vici*. Lisette was under no impression Franklin was a scholar of Ancient Rome. Someone probably told him the meaning of the quote attributed to Julius Caesar, and it had understandably stuck.

"I came, I saw, I conquered," Lisette Darling muttered to herself as she looked out of the car window.

It didn't exactly inspire confidence in Lisette's decision to accept the invitation to join the party taking place on Franklin's yacht that weekend. It was no secret that Franklin liked pretty things. One of those pretty things,

Verity Vance, would be celebrating her twenty-first birthday during the weekend trip. Lisette had seen enough photos of Franklin's latest love interest to note the comparisons between Verity and herself, even if blonde hair and blue eyes were a dime a dozen in Hollywood.

Still, there were lingering feelings of confusion, suspicion, and outright dread that ate at Lisette's sensibilities.

"What if it's a trap?" she'd asked Herbert "Herbie" Hinkle, her boss, the resident fixer at Olympus Studios.

"Then I trust you more than anyone to sniff it out."

She was pleased he put so much trust in her. Winthorpe Media had almost partnered with (or tried to purchase?) Olympus Studios. Perhaps Franklin was making another attempt. Then why invite Lisette instead of Mortimer or Evelyn Huxley, the husband and wife who owned the studios?

No, it couldn't be strictly business. Lisette wasn't high enough up the echelon of power for that.

Which meant this was strictly pleasure.

Having worked in Hollywood for several years now, Lisette was used to being flirted with, pawed at, inappropriately solicited, and even physically "entangled." She always managed to disentangle herself from most of it without help or spilling blood. Sometimes all it took was a swift knee to the proper anatomical zone. She wondered how that would work when trapped on a boat for the weekend.

The car Franklin had sent for her came to a stop. She closed her eyes and took a breath, straightening her shoulders to brace herself preemptively.

"We're here, Miss Darling," the driver said, opening her door for her.

Lisette's eyes flashed open. She considered the young man with an assessing look.

"How much have you heard about this yacht trip?"

"Only that it's one of the swankiest parties this weekend." He sported a smile of envy. "I wouldn't mind trading places with you."

"Careful what you wish for," she said as she stepped out of the car. "So you don't know of anything...interesting or unusual planned for the festivities?"

"The birthday party for Miss Vance? I only know what I read in the papers, but that only means it'll be a zinger."

"A zinger, huh?" Lisette laughed. "Well, it's a good thing I packed my dancing shoes."

Blessedly, her best shoes were black. The theme of the weekend was Black & White, as in everyone had to wear one of each color and no others. That at least made it easy to pack. Who didn't own something in each color?

Even with such a basic color palate, Lisette had enough nice things to wear to match her peers for the weekend. The head of costuming at Olympus Studios gave her access to all her patterns and always made sure there was enough fabric left over for Lisette to snatch. Her roommate Darcy Pembry, had learned to expertly sew from her grandmother. Between the two of them, both relatively the same size and build, they shared a wardrobe that would make most women envious. A few of her better dresses were in the suitcase the driver carried along the dock behind her.

For boarding, she wore a white dress with sheer black, polka-dotted sleeves. Her sunhat was black with white ribbon trim, and her gloves were white with black edges. It all fit the theme perfectly.

Her black dress shoes, good for both dining, dancing, and dashing, should the need arise, clacked down the dock to the boat. Lisette just hoped she didn't break a heel, as they were the only shoes she'd brought. After all, it would only be a short weekend trip. If that was the worst thing that happened, she'd consider it a win.

CHAPTER THREE

LISETTE WALKED up the gangplank to the man in a white uniform with a black bow tie. He was holding a tray of small coupe glasses in one hand. Each contained a hazy pale cocktail with white foam. Sprinkled on top were...poppy seeds?

"I suppose this is in line with the Black & White theme of the weekend, but what is it?" Lisette asked, taking a glass.

"A Black & White Swan, a creation of Miss Vance." His face gave nothing away regarding his opinion of the drink.

Lisette took a hesitant sip and found it was just a White Lady. The poppy seeds were purely for decor, a reason to give the drink its own name. As she drank, Lisette found herself having to spit them out like bits of sand in her drink. Usually drink garnishes weren't such a little nuisance.

Another uniformed man took the suitcase from her driver. Lisette thanked him and tipped a dollar she couldn't afford. She reassured herself that she wouldn't be paying for any meals for the next two days. She hoped he wouldn't feel stiffed having to chauffeur one of the poorer passengers boarding Franklin's yacht. She knew for a fact Lennie

Lamar, one of the top comedic actors in Hollywood and a fellow passenger for the weekend, was well known to be an obscenely generous tipper.

He thanked her with a broad grin and tipped his hat, then left with a jaunty spring in his step. In these times, just having a job was something worth celebrating, she supposed. The Hoovervilles on the outskirts of Los Angeles were a testament to that.

It was also a reminder of how lucky Lisette herself was to be boarding this yacht. If this was a trap, her driver was correct, it was as swanky a trap as they came. There were far worse ways to get ensnared. As such, she happily stuck a cork in her mental complaints and merrily sipped her Black & White Swan—avoiding the irritable poppy seeds as best she could—as she followed the gentleman carrying her suitcase.

It wasn't easy finding her sea legs while sipping a cocktail but Lisette managed, though she nearly splatted while walking down the steps to the cabin areas. They continued down a narrow hall until he reached the correct door and knocked.

"Come in!" It was a woman's voice in a high falsetto.

Lisette wasn't surprised she'd be sharing a room overnight. After all, even a yacht this size could only accommodate so many people. The few people she knew were coming were certainly higher in status than she was.

The man holding her suitcase opened the door for her and she entered first. She had only a moment to process just how tiny the cabin was before she was assaulted in a shower of black and white.

"Welcome!" Two young women in outfits that looked like something from a song and dance chorus line pierced her ears with the greeting. Party horns joined the cacophony and the rain of confetti. Their costumes were essentially black, backless sequined swimsuits with white sailor collars. They wore flesh-colored stockings and heeled shoes.

"Oh, you can just put her case next to that bed," the blonde one said, pointing to the third one crammed behind the door. They weren't even beds really, just cots with nice linens. Considering her years in college at USC and the culture of illegal drinking that might as well have been its own course of study for most of the students, Lisette had definitely spent the night in worse accommodations.

The two girls were still giddy, picking up clumps of confetti to toss into the air again. The man who'd brought her suitcase offered Lisette a grin that seemed to say "good luck," before he tipped his hat and left.

"Hiya!" The pretty brunette greeted Lisette with a saucy grin. She flipped her wavy bob out of one eye. "I'm Bethany Ford, but everyone just calls me Betts. That one over there," she pointed to the other, "is Patticakes."

"Patricia Cresswell," the blonde woman corrected with a pout. "But you can call me Patti."

Patti was around the same age as Betts, but wasn't quite as pretty, with a softer chin, fuller cheeks, and a small overbite. But she had beautiful large blue eyes, enough to make Bette Davis's turn green with envy. Her blonde hair was much longer than Lisette's, falling down past her shoulders in full, fluffy waves.

"We're both good friends of Verity's," Patti continued. "Though Betts has known her longer than I have."

"In other words, I know where all the bodies are buried," Betts said with a wink and a laugh.

"I'm Lisette Darling. I guess we're roommates for the next two days," Lisette said brightly before plucking a poppy seed from her tongue. She looked around the tiny cabin, with a single porthole providing a view of the water.

"I know, it's tiny, ain't it? You'da thought Winthorpe could spring for more," Betts said. "Of course Verity has the big cabin, which is a good thing considering she brought a ton of luggage along. It's right next to Frankie-wanky's, with all sorts of secret access no one else knows about. He's such a sneaky dog."

"This cabin is just fine," Patti said, blushing at her friend's insinuation.

"*Patricia* is one to talk," Betts said in a sardonic manner, rolling her eyes—Lisette wasn't sure what that meant. Betts then brightened up again. "Besides, it ain't like we're gonna be spending any time in here. This weekend is gonna be absolutely tango!"

"Tango?"

"Betts is trying to make that into a word," Patti said with a smirk.

"What? Tango is sexy and fun. It works. Absolutely tango!" Betts grabbed what was left of Lisette's drink and finished it off. She quickly began coughing, working her tongue around to force out the clots of poppy seeds. "Ugh, what was Verity thinkin' with this drink? It would be perfect without those little black specks on top."

"Come on, and let's get a real drink," Patti said with a giggle, as she took Lisette's hand and led her out. "Hey, gorgeous dress. Where'd you get it?"

It was a good thing Lisette hadn't removed her hat and gloves as Patti had her instantly whisked away back outside into the sun.

"Say, didja know Lennie Lamar is here?" Betts said before Lisette could answer Patti. She hooked her arm through Lisette's free one. "That should make things fun."

Betts and Patti giggled conspiratorially, as though there was some joke Lisette wasn't privy to.

"It should give that Joann Golden something to write about," Patti said with a gleeful laugh.

"She's attending as well?" Lisette had learned this beforehand and was looking forward to meeting her. Her question was designed to get an explanation for the guest list.

"Oh, yes."

Lisette was of course familiar with the comedic author of jokes, monologues, and even a script or two that tiptoed along the line of decency. Mostly, Miss Golden had a wicked way with innuendos, which had given her the label, Bardess of Burlesque. Mae West had even used her witty talent for words to help script some of her bawdy delights. She always had audiences roaring with laughter and the censorship boards scratching their heads.

"Verity picked the guest list herself," Patti said. "She has some big plans to be a comedy actress."

That had Lisette wrinkling her brow in confusion even more. She had never personally met Verity Vance and couldn't imagine why she would want her on board for her birthday party. An invitation from Franklin, at least tenuously made sense. One from Verity made no sense at all. Before she could ask, the two continued.

"Then there's the head of Titan Studios, though that's Franklin's invite. Imagine conducting business while our gal is turning twenty-one!"

While the two of them pouted and groused over that, the wheels in Lisette's head were rapidly spinning. Geoff Dreyfus, the head of Titan Studios, was going to be in attendance? While most studios typically got along in a cordially competitive way, Geoff and Mortimer might as well have been mortal enemies. The running theme of Greek mythology was often used as a barb thrown back and forth. The press loved it, not so much everyone else in Hollywood, especially the actors and actresses who were often used as pawns or bartering chips in the petty games of studio heads.

"Who else is coming that you know of?" Lisette asked in an idle tone.

"Hmm, let's see..." Patti said thoughtfully.

"Troy Turner!" Betts exclaimed. "Oh boy, would I love twenty minutes with him."

"Don't be vulgar, Betts," Patti said, then giggled. "At least not until we've had a few gimlets!"

"I don't mean like that, silly. But he's the hottest director in town! You just know he was invited to get Verity into one of his comedies. Happy Birthday, indeed. I'm just sayin' why not spread the wealth a little, huh?"

Lisette knew Troy was coming. Frankly, she wouldn't have been surprised if Betts *had* meant it in the most unsavory way. He was quite handsome, but also brilliant at comedies. Every film he had directed was box office gold. Audiences, who often paid no attention to the director attached, would line up just knowing he had directed a film. Olympus had been trying to secure an exclusive contract with him for ages. That now seemed unlikely if Titan and Winthorpe were forming some sort of partnership and inviting him along for the ride.

"Then there's poor Nevie," Betts said.

"Nevie?" Lisette repeated.

"Neville Frost," Patti replied.

The name was vaguely familiar to Lisette. "He's a producer, no?"

"Yep," Betts said. "He and Verity go back a long ways." She leaned in to whisper in confidence. "He ain't been so lucky lately. I think she's throwin' him a bone, hoping Mr. Dreyfus or Franklin will pick up one of the movies he's tryin' to produce."

"Unfortunately Cynthia is here with him," Patti said. The way Betts instantly joined her in groaning confirmed neither was a fan of the woman. "Talk about a wet blanket."

"Here we are!" Betts announced as they reached the top deck, where one or two of the big names already mingled. In a corner behind the long bar, she could barely see a jazz quartet filling the air with music that had just the right amount of liveliness to create a celebratory air.

Lisette noticed Lennie Lamar right away. The outlandishly long limbs that provided their own form of comedy, stumbling and tumbling across the screen, were attached to a similarly noodle-like body that leaned against the railing, staring wistfully out to sea. In a cheeky nod to the theme, he wore a casual white polo shirt with a formal black bowtie. He had on white wide-legged pants with a black belt and black dress shoes. A jaunty white sailor hat sat at an angle on his head making the amusing outfit look perfectly silly. Both girls dragged Lisette over.

"Hiya, Lennie!" Betts squealed.

A mask instantly appeared, transforming that pensive look on his face into something more impish. "How's it tweetin', my little chickadees?" He said in a zany voice out the side of his mouth, as he held an imaginary cigar. Both girls laughed and clapped.

"Oh you," Patti said, genuinely smitten.

"And who is this little goldfinch?" He looked at Lisette appreciatively.

"She's our roommate for the weekend."

"You don't say?" That was all the innuendo anyone needed, the joke wrote itself. However, Lisette thought he might change his tune if he saw the haphazard way their beds had been thrown together in the tiny room. Not much space for innuendo to become reality. Which was just fine with Lisette.

"We're gonna go get drinks and be back in two shakes," Betts said, giving him a kittenish wave. She dragged both Lisette and Patti away to the bar.

Joann Golden was already there ordering a glass of vodka. "No ice, no lemon, no nothin'! I like my drinks like I like my men, neat and naughty." She wore an outlandishly large black sunhat atop the bright red hair that was her trademark. She wore a white dress which her voluptuous body filled out quite daringly. Even at over fifty, she had no inhibitions about flaunting herself.

She turned her attention to the newest arrivals and one side of her mouth hitched up with amusement. "Old Frankie is going to get himself into trouble this weekend," she said in a voice heavily etched with the years of cigarette smoking that she had started long before it was acceptable for women to smoke in public. She was old enough to be cynical about almost everything—and get away with calling Franklin "Frankie." He notoriously hated the condensed version of his name.

"It's a pleasure to meet you, Miss Golden," Lisette said, thrilled to meet the woman in person.

"Miss Golden? Gosh, honey, you make me feel like my knickers are made of gold. Joann will do just fine," she said, taking Lisette's offered hand. She had a robust shake. She studied Lisette through narrowed eyes. "You're that gal who does Herbie Hinkle's job for him."

"Well, I wouldn't say—"

Before she could finish, Joann coughed out a laugh, which erupted into a short coughing fit. When she recovered she waved a hand Lisette's way. "I'm just joshin' you, honey. I know Old Herbie has earned his stripes. What's your name, anyway?"

"Lisette Darling."

Joann paused. "You're kidding me."

Lisette felt her face flush, used to people reacting to her overly precious last name. "I'm afraid not."

"Well, you might as well own it, sweetheart. One thing I've learned in this town is that it's better to have men think you're some cutesy, dumb redhead—or blonde in your case—and take 'em for all they're worth, than have them charging in, guns blazing because they know what a lioness you are. It's too late for me, of course. Too many men wear the scars of my claw marks." She grinned. "Some of 'em in places the sun don't shine."

Lisette laughed along with her, liking her even more. Betts and Patti joined in.

"Well, good luck to ya this weekend, Darling. Me thinks you're gonna need it." Joann looked past Lisette's shoulder. "Speak of the devil—or should I say succubus."

Lisette turned to find Verity on the arm of Franklin, both of them finishing their ascent to the top deck. She was stricken by just how eerily familiar Verity looked, as though Lisette was looking in a mirror. Her hair was almost the same shade of blonde and cropped short in exactly the same way. She was also the same height, though a bit more curvaceous in the hips. Even their facial features had the same blue eyes, high cheekbones, pencil-thin eyebrows, and an identical shade of lip color. The only subtle differences were Verity's chin, which was a bit more pointed, and a slightly more button-like nose.

The birthday girl looked around at the few people who had already joined them on the top deck. When her eyes landed on Lisette, they briefly narrowed. She wondered if the same thoughts were running through Verity's head about how similar they looked. But her expression quickly transformed, her face radiating a broad smile as she released Franklin and walked over to greet Lisette.

"Why look at this," Verity said, taking both hands of a quite stunned Lisette. "We're practically twins!"

CHAPTER FOUR

"Gosh, you two really do look like twins!" Patti stared back and forth between Lisette and Verity, who still held both her hands in hers.

"Well, she has a much better dress than I do," Verity said, the dazzling smile on her face fading a bit as she eyed what Lisette was wearing.

"Yours is gorgeous, Verity. Absolutely tango," Betts said.

A pert smile came to Verity's face at the compliment. She lowered her lids demurely to look at the dress she wore. Lisette had seen women wear leopard print and even giraffe, but zebra print was a new one. It was fashionably cut with a billowing skirt that the sea breeze picked up. Still, it did fit with the theme of the weekend. What was more black and white than a zebra?

"I suppose I have you to thank for inviting me?" Lisette asked, hoping she would give an explanation.

"Don't think anything of it, Lisette—can I call you that?"

"Of course."

"And call me Verity. We're going to have such a fun weekend!"

"I look forward to it. I guess I'm just wondering why—"

"And look at you two!" Verity interrupted, instantly shifting her attention to Patti and Betts. "The absolute bee's knees! I knew those outfits would look darling on you. I think Mr. Turner will think so too," she said with a wink.

Lisette watched Verity hook her arms through those of each of her friends and walk them away.

"Sly as a fox," Joann mused, obviously noting how easily Verity avoided the question Lisette was about to ask. She picked up the cigarette holder she had set down to accept her drink. After sticking it in her mouth she squinted one eye at Lisette and added, "I believe the female of that species is called a vixen."

Lisette had a feeling it was a fitting label, though she didn't want to say so out loud. That sense she was being led right into a trap only became stronger. What was Verity's game?

Lisette shifted her attention to Franklin. He'd been accosted by Hedley Harper, who had just made an appearance. She wore a tastefully tailored white dress with black buttons, collar, and belt. The hat on her head was black, with netting that seemed more fitting for a funeral. But together it made the Hollywood tabloid journalist (if one could even call her that) seem almost as sophisticated as she wanted the world to think she was.

If Lisette was going to get answers, those two were the most likely candidates. After all, she was a fixer. Best to put out fires before they began.

Hedley was the first to note Lisette's approach. Whatever it was she had been urgently discussing with a reluctant Franklin, she immediately ceased, straightening up and greeting the interloper with a coy smile.

"Why Lisette Darling, such a pleasure to see you, as always," Hedley said, that mid-Atlantic lofty tone she had so carefully cultivated accenting each word with precision.

"Is it?" Lisette replied, one eyebrow arched with cynicism. "You only seem to call or visit when you want to use me for information. Sadly I have none to give today."

"She's such a cynical little thing," Hedley said to Franklin.

"Speaking of both cynicism and information, I do have to wonder why I was invited this weekend?" Lisette said directly to Franklin. "I would have thought I'd be persona non grata after our last interaction."

"Water under the bridge," he said with a laugh, waving that old business away.

"That's good to hear, but I'm still a bit bewildered."

"Verity said she was fascinated by you is all." He winked at Lisette. "I think she wants to make sure you intend to stay firmly behind the scenes in this business. No need for the competition in front of the camera, you see."

"You do bear a striking resemblance," Hedley said, the sides of her mouth turned down to ponder it.

"Exactly," Franklin said with a grin. He winked at Lisette again. "Expect to become her best friend this weekend."

Lisette doubted that would happen. She already had the sense that Verity enjoyed a certain type of friend, and Lisette wasn't very fond of being manipulated. However, her hypocritical side wasn't above doing the manipulating. She might as well dig for information while she had access.

"I understand Geoff Dreyfus will be here this weekend. Don't tell me you're turning poor Verity's birthday into a business deal," she said in the sort of coquettish voice she knew a man like Franklin would appreciate.

"Why Lisette Darling, you're as shameless as I am," Hedley said with a hint of admiration in her voice. That, of course, ruined the ruse.

A placid, knowing smile curled Franklin's mouth. "This is a birthday weekend, Miss Darling. Why not simply enjoy the festivities? My Verity's got a few fun things planned for us, and I know I'm looking forward to it." His eyes settled on someone obviously more interesting than Lisette. "If you'll excuse me."

She watched him head towards Lennie, to whom Verity had dragged her two friends.

"I do believe he's actually in love this time," Hedley said with a surprising trace of sentimentality.

"She's over half his age."

"That would hardly be a first. But I think it would be good for him to finally settle down."

Lisette watched Verity do a little can-can, lifting her skirt high enough to see her garters. "Are we sure she's the settling type?"

If Hedley had a response, it was thwarted by the arrival of Troy Turner.

"It seems I came right in the middle of the first act!" His voice boomed and every eye on the top deck turned to look as he headed straight to Verity. He wore a white jacket over a black dress shirt with white pants. Verity stopped dancing and accepted a kiss on each cheek, both of which were pink with pleasure.

Lisette couldn't blame her. Troy was tall and finely built, filling out his white jacket with a perfect V shape. His dark hair was combed straight back, showing off a high forehead, razor-sharp nose, and fine mouth. Even the pencil mustache, which Lisette usually hated, didn't do him a disservice.

"I suppose we know who is starring in his next movie then."

"Do you ever stop working, Miss Darling?"

"It's just a theory. Unless, of course, you know something I don't?"

"That would be a rare treat for once," Hedley said with a laugh.

Lisette joined with a chuckle. There would be plenty of time for information gathering during the next forty-eight hours. She might as well relax and enjoy herself for now.

"Join me for a drink why don't you? I need something to wash these horrid poppy seeds out of my mouth," Hedley said, her lips twisted with displeasure.

Seeing as how she'd only been able to enjoy half of her Black and White Swan before Betts finished it off, Lisette walked with Hedley to the bar. They each ordered a glass of white wine and stood with Joann to observe Verity with her guests. She was doing another flirtatious dance, focusing on all three men, one at a time.

"All she needs is a cake to pop out of and there's the second act right there," Joann said around the cigarette holder in her mouth, punctuating that with a cackle. "She's more blatant than some of the acts I wrote for the Minsky Brothers. And good old LaGuardia is doin' his best to shut those down back in New York."

"That's the influence of Hollywood," Hedley said proudly. "Hayes and his code have finally reached the East Coast."

"Fortunately, we have our own little burlesque show right here," Joann said.

Lisette saw it as a bit of harmless fun. In another time,

she would have been right next to Verity, doing the same thing. Franklin obviously liked that his little star was the center of attention. Some men considered that a reflection of themselves. Today, Lisette was happy to sip her wine and observe from afar.

Her eye was caught by a couple entering the deck. They didn't arrive quite as boisterously as the others had. In fact, they seemed rather hesitant. The man already had his white hat in hand and the mouth of the woman with him was preemptively turned down, as though finding fault with everything around her.

"I suppose every party needs a pooper," Joann observed, looking at the couple with disfavor.

"Neville Frost," Lisette said.

"And his wife Cynthia. She certainly married a man with a fitting last name to give her. That woman could freeze a polar bear's—"

"Now, now, Joann, they can hear you," Hedley said smiling at the couple as they neared the bar instead of inter-rupting Verity's little act. "Neville, how are you! And Cynthia, that's such a lovely black dress. I suppose you are the black to his white? How very clever!"

Cynthia looked more like she was attending a wake, in Lisette's opinion. Her dour expression, even in the face of such a warm greeting, didn't help. She was pretty in a willowy way that didn't wear misery very attractively. Her thin, blonde hair was similar in color to Lisette's though her frail curls didn't seem to be holding up well against the ocean breeze.

Neville was handsome in a boyish way that wouldn't do him any favors now that he seemed to be well past thirty. Still, there was a gentleness in his features—wavy brown hair, kind blue eyes, and a cherubic smile above a sharp chin —that allowed women to let down their guard.

"I know Verity is thrilled you were able to come. It'll be such a fun weekend, don't you think?"

"You're laying it on a bit thick, Hedley," Cynthia said.

The smile on Hedley's face froze in surprise. Although Lisette agreed with Cynthia—usually Hedley's fawning affectations were reserved for those who could benefit her somehow—it had been a rude retort.

"Cynthia, not now," Neville hissed, a hint of a soft southern drawl in his voice. "At least try to enjoy this weekend."

She met her husband with a level gaze. "We shouldn't even be here. This ridiculous theme, those awful drinks, and who knows what else she has planned? Just look at her, flaunting herself. Agreeing to this was a mistake."

The three women near them stared with uncomfortable curiosity. Why did she seem to despise Verity so?

Neville wasn't inclined to give an answer, instead taking her hand and dragging her toward Verity, who suddenly noticed their arrival.

"Nevie!" The birthday girl threw her arms open and snaked them around Neville's neck so hard the two of them nearly toppled over. She completely ignored Cynthia. "I'm so glad you came. Now all my oldest and dearest friends are here!"

"Yes, yes, this should work out well," Hedley said, mostly to herself. Lisette eyed her and found a strained smile on her face. The only time Lisette had seen Hedley troubled over something was when her arch-enemy Lorlene Divine got a story before her. Lisette slid her eyes to Joann on the other side of Hedley, who looked just as puzzled by the journalist's sudden bout of agitation.

Lisette returned her attention to Neville, who was greeting everyone in Verity's orbit. They all seemed pleasant enough now. Even Cynthia had finally managed a hint of a smile.

"Ah, our last arrival is here," Hedley observed, back to her old self again.

Lisette followed her gaze to see Geoff Dreyfus standing at the top of the stairs leading to the upper deck. He wore a tuxedo jacket with a white silk lapel. He was short in stature, but carried himself like the industry giant that he was. It was fitting he would be the last to arrive, as he was probably the most important man there, save for Franklin. In fact, Lisette noticed a sudden hush that came over everyone, as though they had stopped to stare in awe.

"And with that, we have act three," Joann said with a humorless laugh.

CHAPTER FIVE

"GEOFF!" Franklin was the first to greet him. He pulled himself away from the crowd surrounding Verity, who looked none too happy by the most recent arrival. Lisette assumed that was because, despite Franklin's assurances, there would be business conducted that weekend.

Geoff stood near the entrance to the upper deck, forcing Franklin to come to him. He seemed reluctant to join the boisterous activity surrounding the birthday girl, staring in her direction with a decidedly grim look on his face. Perhaps he too objected to conducting business during a birthday celebration.

The two titans of industry removed themselves to a corner, and Verity decided to bring all eyes back to her. With the help of Lennie, who looked perfectly besotted with the lovely blonde, she stood precariously on the lowest rung of the railings.

"Silence everyone!" She frowned and glared in the direction of the jazz band, who apparently didn't stop playing quickly enough for her. Once they were quiet, she plastered on a bright smile. "I want to thank all of you for coming out to celebrate my birthday. It's the big two-one. Gosh, I feel so old!"

That got the expected laughs and titters from her friends and playful groans from everyone else.

"If she's old, I'm the rotting mummy of Cleopatra."

Lisette laughed, this time genuinely.

Hedley turned to them with a frown. "Don't be macabre, Joann."

"Franklin!" Verity called out, a slight edge to the kittenish lilt in her voice. "Isn't it time we set off to sea?"

That was obviously more of a demand than a question. Franklin and Geoff finished what little bit they had to discuss, not caring that all eyes were on them now. After a minute—Verity knew better than to interrupt again—he pulled away. The master of ceremonies smile was back on.

"Welcome, everyone!" He opened his arms wide as though presenting the grand opening of a circus. Lisette wondered how far from the truth that would be. "It's going to be a fun-filled weekend on the Pacific. At midnight tonight, our own Verity turns twenty-one, and we're going to ring it in with style."

He walked over and threw an arm around Verity's waist. She laughed and fell into his chest. He swung her around and then set her down to walk over to a bell behind the bar. He gave it a good hard ring, and a clang pealed so loudly that Lisette felt the urge to childishly cover her ears. That must have been the cue to the captain because half a minute later, they all heard a distant motor and the boat began to move.

"Come, come!" Verity said, urging everyone to follow her to the stairs. "We have an early lunch set up on the back deck."

Lisette waited for her betters to precede her. Betts and

Patti were first, dragging Troy with them. Lennie followed with a wry smile. Cynthia had pulled Neville aside to have a quick, angry word with him.

"Shall we, ladies? I, for one, feel like being reminded of my mortality over rubbery chicken" Joann said, tapping the cigarette at the end of her holder into an ashtray.

"I plan on having fun," Hedley said briskly, a mild hint of admonishment in her voice.

"I suppose I'll settle somewhere in the middle of those two things," Lisette said with a grin.

The three of them descended the stairs heading to the landing at the stern of the yacht. It was big enough to hold a large round table that sat all twelve of them. There was an awning shading everyone from the sun. It was a fine Southern California day, but the last thing anyone wanted was a sunburn to top off the weekend.

Betts had made sure to snag the chair next to Troy. Verity had probably insisted her friends sit on either side of her, which meant Patti was the unlucky gal out. That left Joann to take the seat on his other side. Lisette sat on her other side. Hedley decided it was wise to take the seat on the far side of the table as close to Franklin as she could get.

The final three members of the birthday guest list arrived at the same time. Lisette was surprised when Geoff took the seat next to her. Neville was smart enough to sit on his other side, which left Cynthia sitting next to Hedley. Neither of them seemed happy about that.

"For a second I thought I was sitting next to the birthday girl," Geoff said, eyeing Lisette with a bemused smile. His eyes crystallized into a look of familiarity, and the smile became a grin. "I know you."

"What a coincidence, I know you," she said with a half-cocked smile.

Geoff laughed. "How is Herbie these days? Tell him we always have an opening for him at Titan should he get the itch."

"So you can scratch all of Olympus's dirty secrets out of his head?"

He laughed again. "I would be stupid not to. You of course are welcome to come as well, Miss Darling."

"If you tell me what you're really doing here this weekend, I might consider it."

He chuckled. "I can see why he likes you. Of course, I'd be smart enough to put you in front of the camera where you belong."

"And I'd be smart enough to say no."

"In which case you really are a smart broad."

"Gee, thanks."

"*Ahem!*" Verity cleared her throat, specifically looking at Geoff and Lisette. When they both turned to give their full attention, a pert smile came to her face. "In honor of my birthday, we're going to start with a toast. Then, we're going to play a little game of telephone, but...you have to change one word of what's whispered to you when you whisper to the next person. I think we have enough comedians to make it funny."

"Forget meeting my maker, this is worse, reliving my childhood," Joann muttered under her breath.

Two waiters brought out six glasses of champagne each and set them down in front of each person. Lisette checked to make sure there wasn't something "unique" in them to keep them on theme.

Verity was still standing and lifted her glass, then waited for everyone else to do the same. "Here's...to *me!*"

"Here, here! There, there!" Lennie shouted, making her

giggle in a self-deprecating way while all the others took a sip.

"Twenty and three-hundred-sixty-four days looks good on you, Verity," Troy said. "I'm curious to see what twenty-one will look like."

She wiggled prettily where she stood and shot Troy a pleased smile. Then, she collected herself and eyed everyone at the table. She made a point of pretending to think of something to say, but far too quickly she leaned over and whispered into Bett's ear.

Betts rolled her eyes and with a prim smile turned to Troy and whispered. Everyone watched as he grinned and then whispered to Joann.

"Why Troy, you do know how to make a girl blush," Joann said, girlishly slapping him on the arm. "Honey, there's only two people I'd let do that to me, my doctor and Mr. Golden. Currently, there's no Mr. Golden, but in your case, I'm accepting offers." She waggled her eyebrows, which had everyone laughing. Verity in particular hopped in place and clapped, pleased that her little game was being received so well.

"What's virile and dumb and read all night," Joann whispered to Lisette. She could guess which word Joann had come up with. Lisette assumed the original sentence had been on theme with the party: What's black and white and read all over. It was a well-known riddle meant to be spoken so one didn't know whether the speaker was saying "read" or "red." The answer, a newspaper, gave away the correct word.

Lisette rolled her eyes thoughtfully, building the anticipation with a smile before she turned to Geoff.

"Someone's virile and dumb and read all night." She couldn't help a small giggle at the silliness of it.

He breathed out a laugh, but was goodnatured about passing on the phrase, his own word inserted. Lisette actually found herself eagerly anticipating what would come out of Patti's mouth at the end. There were chuckles, expressions of confusion, and shakes of the head. Finally, it was Lennie's turn to repeat to Patti what had been said to him, one word changed.

"Mickey Mouse is silly and chocolate not blue every summer?" Patti said, with a look of utter puzzlement on her face.

Everyone, especially those early on in the game laughed.

"Good grief, that ain't even the right number of words!" Betts said. "Someone really messed up."

"Or deliberately sabotaged it," Verity said with a kittenish pout.

"Okay, you have to tell me the original sentence. Just how badly did we do here?" Franklin asked.

"What's black and white and read all over!" Verity said, Betts and Troy joining in, as they had been early enough in the game to know.

"But no reading on this trip, we're here to have fun!" Verity said in a babyish voice, wagging her finger from side to side.

"Speaking of not reading, I suppose this is where I should announce a little birthday surprise I have for you, Verity."

Verity's eyes glittered with delight at Franklin's announcement. "*Ohh*, what is it?"

"I have created a little—or perhaps not so little—reel of your entire film career. Every role you've played, every scene you've been in, no matter how small, I've managed to obtain it. Let me tell you, some were not so easy to come by! But I managed. I had someone put them all into a single reel for us to view after lunch in the screening room on board. There will even be popcorn."

"Why Franklin, I...I don't know quite what to say." Verity looked flustered at the grand gesture. Her smile was decidedly forced.

Lisette sympathized. Many an actress had started out either less practiced than they were later on or forced into roles they wouldn't have dreamed of taking once they had top billing. Verity hadn't risen quite that high yet and still had to prove herself. It was awfully negligent of Franklin to gather all her roles to present to an audience as important as this one without giving her notice, let alone without editorial power.

Franklin must have sensed Verity wasn't entirely happy with his announcement. "Not to worry, darling, you're fabulous in every scene. Even when only saying one word, you're far superior to some of the most notable actresses in this city."

A mask dropped and Verity became the giggling blonde he preferred. She rushed over and hugged him. "Oh, you're just the sweetest!"

Lisette wasn't fooled. Still, there was no point in biting the hand that fed you. Even if Verity's earlier performances were disasters, Franklin had the power to put her in front of the camera in a starring role. Wasn't that the point of the entire weekend celebration?

"But for now, it looks like the buffet is set up just inside so help yourself," Franklin announced.

Lisette felt her stomach growl at the enticing smells coming from inside. Contrary to Joann's prediction, Franklin Winthorpe wasn't one to serve rubbery chicken.

She wouldn't have been surprised if he hired a gourmet chef specifically for the two days they were at sea.

As she rose, she saw Cynthia pull Neville aside to whisper something urgent to him. He reached out a hand to place on her arm in an attempt to settle her. She shook it off and hissed something at him. Betts and Patti had been right about her. Thus far, she had been a bit of a wet blanket. What could be so important she had to complain to her husband, yet again?

As for Lisette, she felt the exact opposite. Her unease was beginning to shed, helped along by a bit of bubbly. Perhaps she'd shake her own curls loose this weekend and have a bit of fun. Thus far, it certainly had been...tango.

CHAPTER SIX

THE REMAINDER of lunch had been quite fun. Cynthia had gotten over whatever had upset her, leading to her fervent conversation with Neville. Joann and Lennie seemed to vie for who could be the funniest. One of the two was certainly the most ribald. If Verity Vance was hoping to be the next Mae West, she had chosen well with Joann.

Lisette had to admit that Verity did have a certain appeal. She had all the men eating out of her hands. Lennie was obviously more than just star-struck, he was in love. Neville always had a certain sentimental look on his face when he stared at her. Geoff's smile was more assessing, as though wondering if that charm would work as well on the silver screen. Even Troy had a certain intensity when he studied her.

Franklin reveled in it.

When it came time for the viewing, Lisette had pled sea sickness and exhaustion. She had no reason to cozy up to either Franklin or Verity. Besides, she had a feeling there wouldn't be much opportunity for sleep that night, especially if Verity's birthday literally fell at midnight.

She had indeed fallen asleep and was woken up by the sound of Betts and Patti noisily returning to the cabin.

"I just don't understand it. I all but wiggled my derrière in Troy's face. How is Verity's bit part in some silly movie more interesting than that!"

Lisette's eyes snapped open in surprise. Watching as they piled in, still in their sparkly sailor costumes.

"See there, you woke our roomie, Betts," Patti said, waving a hand Lisette's way.

A tired smile appeared on Lisette's face. "It's fine. I should be waking up anyway. What time is it?"

"Almost time for dinner," Patti said.

"Really?" Lisette looked out the porthole and saw it was twilight. "Goodness, I must have been more tired than I thought."

"Don't worry, you didn't miss much." Betts fell onto her cot in a huff.

"I thought it was nice, Franklin doing that for her. You would have thought she'd be a bit more grateful about it."

"When has she ever thanked anyone?" Betts groused.

"He even showed films I didn't remember she was in."

"Yeah, yeah, she's been in lotsa movies. Even an entire speaking role with Lennie Lamar." She smirked in an ironic manner. "But look at her now. You'd think with so many big names on the boat, Verity would do her part to throw us a bone, wouldn'tcha?"

"They call it hustling for a reason," Lisette said with a sympathetic smile.

"Besides, it's *her* birthday, Betts," Patti said.

"I oughta find my own butter and egg man. Then, he could just buy my way into a role like Verity's Franklin is doin'."

"Rich men aren't easy to come by these days."

Betts scowled at Patti. "You don't say?"

Patti looked abashed, her cheeks coloring as she turned away.

"Don't tell me Franklin is partnering with Titan Studios just to get Verity a starring role," Lisette asked in a joking tone. She figured she might as well pry where she could.

Betts shrugged with disinterest and fell back on her bed. "Who knows?"

Patti's eyes deftly darted away again and she nibbled her bottom lip as she rifled through her suitcase. That was interesting. At least Lisette knew which of the two was the best pressure point, not that she planned on making a nuisance of herself that weekend. If the companies did merge, it would be in the papers soon enough. Mortimer Huxley had had his chance with Winthorpe Media and dropped the ball. Probably for the best.

Lisette turned her attention to her dress for dinner that evening. The dress she'd worn to board had been chosen to deliberately make a striking first impression. For dinner, she thought she'd go a bit more formal, yet understated. It was a long, white, sleeveless, backless silk dress paired with black bangles and a black sash at the waist.

Betts and Patti had changed and accompanied her to the dining room. The former wore a black silky dress with two thin straps crossing her back, and a white feathered headband. Patti wore a lovely dress that looked rather expensive, done in a sequined black and white harlequin pattern. In the dining room, the jazz quartet from earlier was more visible. They sat in a corner playing some mellow tunes that filled the air with pleasant background music.

"Hmm, black and white indeed," Betts said eyeing the band with a small laugh.

Lisette wondered if the contrasting race between the

party guests and the band—all dressed in white tuxedos—was planned or just a coincidence. Patti giggled shyly and gave a wiggle of the fingers. The trumpet player winked back playfully as he played a low tune.

On one side of the large room, there was a long table with place cards, should anyone get it into their head to choose their own dining neighbor. Franklin and Verity had place cards at either end. Lisette was surprisingly placed right next to Franklin. Verity either didn't feel threatened by how much she resembled her, or she trusted that Lisette wouldn't try to use that to her advantage and make any moves toward stealing him. Since she had never met the woman before this weekend, Lisette assumed it was the former. Patti sat directly across from her with Lennie on her left. Finishing off that side were Joann, Cynthia, then Troy, right next to Verity. On Lisette's side of the table, she sat next to Betts, then Hedley, Neville, and ending with Geoff on Verity's other side. Neville was probably pleased about his seat placement if he really was looking for someone to help produce his work.

"Do you see?" Betts whispered to Lisette as they took their seats. "Verity's made darn sure all the meat is at her end, leaving us the gristle and fat."

Her voice had been wisely low enough such that poor Lennie across from them didn't hear. He was hardly gristle or fat, even beyond his long lean body. He and Patti were having a seemingly enjoyable conversation. Lisette looked down the table at the others, at least those she could see. Joann smoked from her cigarette holder, looking bored. Cynthia's mouth was still firmly puckered with disapproval. Troy was focused on the band, tuning everyone else out as he enjoyed the music.

Everyone except Franklin and Verity had arrived. The men were less imaginative when it came to dinner attire, all of them in similar black tuxedos. Joann wore a lush white number trimmed in fur, her only black accessory the cigarette holder in her hand. Cynthia had transitioned to white for the evening, chiffon with overly large ruffles as sleeves that were fading in fashion.

A waiter walked around with a tray of Black & White Swans. Joann was practical enough to take one, then scoop the poppy seed-dotted foam away with a spoon before sipping. Everyone else took note and opted to accept a glass and do the same. Only Lisette, Troy, and Cynthia refrained. Lisette figured there would be plenty of wine and champagne later, and she wanted to enjoy herself, not get sloppy drunk.

Franklin and Verity eventually arrived arm in arm, looking regal. Verity was in a wrap-style dress that was white on one side and black on the other. Franklin was in a nicely tailored, but otherwise unremarkable tuxedo. They each took their respective ends of the table.

Franklin remained standing next to Lisette and reached out to ring a little bell that sat next to his plate. Instantly, two waiters appeared. One took the Black & White Swans, which were by then finished, and the other brought champagne-filled glasses.

Franklin lifted his glass toward Verity. "A very happy birthday to you, my sweet."

Lisette, like everyone else, was happy to learn that was the sum total of his speech. Everyone lifted their glasses and shouted "Happy Birthday!" While the band played a jazzy version of "Happy Birthday to You," they all drank.

Franklin sat down and the first serving arrived. Lisette

assumed she had been seated next to him for a reason, so she waited to see what bit of information he wanted to get from her. Instead, he turned to Lennie on the other side of Patti.

"Verity tells me you're one of the first famous people she met when she first set foot in Hollywood." There was some underlying tone in his voice that hinted it was more than just an idle icebreaker.

"She was. I helped her get that part in *Happy Times*. It's a shame she didn't have more of a role in it. She played her character perfectly."

"All ten seconds of it," Betts said with a snort.

"Ten seconds is ten seconds," Patti said with a disapproving frown.

"That depends on what you do with those ten seconds," Joann said with a chuckle.

"Yes, yes, well, naturally we want to focus on bigger roles for her in the future." Franklin admired Verity from afar. "She's gonna be a star, I tell ya."

It seemed Betts was right about landing a wealthy man. Verity had gone and landed one who had some very fine connections. A top director and the head of a major studio on either side of her was quite the advantage.

"Stars shine brightest just before they go boom," Betts muttered into her champagne glass, making a popping sound with her lips. "Verity should probably—"

"Say, did anyone see the recent news about that monster they found in a loch over in Scotland? Apparently, she found herself a boy dinosaur and they now have a family." Lennie interrupted. An exaggerated look of discontent came to his face. "I tell ya, mythical creatures are making more whoopee than me. What's the world coming to!"

That had everyone on their end of the table laughing,

even Betts. Lisette hadn't missed the way Lennie had masterfully shifted the topic of discussion away from whatever Betts was about to say.

"Oh Lennie, you always make the most sordid observations," Hedley chided, though in a good-natured tone.

"What are you all discussing down there that's so funny?" Verity asked.

"Lennie was just telling us about the Loch Ness Monster's new family," Hedley answered.

"Has she been adopted?"

"She's been corrupted, Miss Vance," Lennie answered. "Defiled by the institution of marriage."

"Did that dynamite that set her free also set loose a pastor dinosaur?" Lisette asked in a wry tone, earning a few chuckles.

"Fair point, Miss Darling. Let us just say, the two have been dancing the tango a little too closely." Lennie paused in thought, then chuckled before continuing with a limerick:

A beast with certain proclivities
That scandalized all the old biddies
With her dinosaur hubby, she'd rub-a-dub-dubby
And now they have twenty-three kiddies.

Everyone at the table erupted with boisterous laughter and clapped with delight at his suggestive limerick.

"I knew inviting you would be a hoot!" Verity exclaimed. Her eyes brightened with an idea. "We should all come up with a limerick! Or at least try to. The best one gets a special treat. What do you say, Franklin?"

"Brilliant, we have a few wits joining us tonight. The best rated gets...well, I'm feeling generous, a full page spread in one of the Winthorpe publications of their choice." That got an immediate reaction from around the table. With national and even international circulation in the millions, that was enough to catapult many a career for those in attendance.

"Does that include us journalists?" Hedley asked, her voice pitched just a note higher with anticipation. Hedley could write the column of her choice, perhaps something serious to catapult her into a better tier of journalism.

"Yes, Hedley, you can write the story of your choice, it may even lead to that extended contract you've been harping about," he answered in a paternalistic tone. Lisette couldn't see her, but she was certain Hedley was beaming. Perhaps that's what she'd been discussing with Franklin earlier, before Lisette interrupted them.

Franklin lifted one finger of warning. "Just a caveat to the winner, I *do* retain editorial discretion."

The soft laughter couldn't mask the buzz of hope and excitement in the air. Would it be a glowing review or a full-page advertisement for a movie? A fashion spread could certainly get eyes on the pretty Betts, a few of them attached to men worth millions and just as influential as Franklin. Lisette could see her face was already contorted in thought.

"Oh, I suppose I'll go first. But if I win, I want a book deal. I feel like writing a good memoir, spill all my dirty secrets," Joann said, giving Franklin a hard look.

"I doubt any such book would make it past the censors," Franklin said, and they both laughed. "Still, I think a good profile might get you what you're after. If there's enough interest, you might even find yourself with a healthy book advance."

"I'm sold," she said with a smirk. She quirked one eyebrow up and a devilish smile came to her face:

A mythical beast in the lake
She'd give the old-timers a quake
She'd make 'em feel spry, so much that they'd die
But they all wore a smile at their wake

With Joann's hoarse voice uttering every word in the most suggestive manner, it had everyone in stitches. Even Cynthia, brought a hand up to hide a reluctant laugh she'd coughed out. Verity seemed particularly pleased with how her idea was panning out.

"Okay, who's next? How about you Troy?"

He breathed out a self-deprecating laugh and waved a hand. Lisette could see that he'd finished off his champagne by then. "I simply direct. Heaven forbid I try to do better than the comedic wit at the table."

"Oh, come on." Verity pouted prettily.

"No, no, I'll allow others their moment to shine. I think it might be a bad idea for Franklin to owe me any favors," he said with a taunting look to the other end of the table. He turned to give Verity a half-cocked smile. "Or you, my dear."

Franklin laughed good-naturedly. "How very magnanimous of you, Troy."

"Oh fine," Verity said, rolling her eyes. She arched a brow toward Neville. Then asked in a hopeful tone, "Surely you have one?"

"I...well, it's probably not on par with the, as you say, comedic wit at the table," he said, sounding nervous.

"You don't have to participate, Neville," Cynthia said

from across the table, a note of disapproval already in her voice.

"Nonsense, we're all friends here," Verity said in a dismissive tone.

Neville took a breath and straightened his shoulders then recited his limerick:

> There once was a monster quite flirty
> She wasn't afraid to get dirty.
> With a bump and a grind, she'd show off her hind
> Then ask, 'Aren't I purty?'

The limerick was good, it was just the way poor Neville had uttered it, ironically like a nervous boy reciting an Easter poem in church. Lisette thought he could have used a bit of direction from Troy, who was busy ordering a glass of wine. Even Verity stared at him with disappointment. Lisette felt a pang of sympathy for him. He, more than anyone at the table, probably could have used some good press.

"May I go next?" Hedley asked in a prim voice.

Verity waved her on and she recited hers:

> There once was a monster named Ness
> Her morals were really a mess
> She'd flirt with a boy, pretend to be coy
> Then hitch up the hem of her dress.

"That's surprisingly tame for you, Hedley," Franklin said.

Lisette agreed, especially considering how dirty she sometimes got in her articles.

"I prefer to be at least *somewhat* a lady in mixed company," Hedley scoffed.

"I have one!" Patti exclaimed.

"Well, well, well, Patticakes has decided to join the fun," Verity said with surprise. "Let's hear what you've got."

After a brief frown at the nickname, Patti's face glowed with renewed glee before she gave her limerick:

> There once was a dino who cha-cha'ed
> And made the boys go ohh-la-*la*-lah
> With a kick in the air, she'd do it with flair
> Then make the boys shame all their mamas

Betts was the first to laugh and slowly clap. "Brava, Patti, very tango! Who knew you had such a wicked streak in you?"

Her applause was joined by everyone else. The laughter that accompanied it diffused the minor cloud of discomfort that had followed Neville's attempt.

Pattie glowed with pleasure.

"Who knew indeed," Verity said, then added. "Though it didn't *exactly* rhyme."

"My turn!" Betts said next to Lisette. She went before anyone could speak:

> There once was a beast in Loch Ness
> She was always good for a "yes."
> If you asked for a show, she'd *never* say no
> But you'd be with ten dollars less.

Betts was certainly one who didn't need any direction from Troy or anyone else. She knew exactly which words to stress and her face exuded flirtation as she shook her shoulders along with each verse. Lisette was impressed. She'd make a fine vixen on the stage once she got her shot.

"For ten dollars she'd better make me breakfast and iron my shirt," Lennie groused, which had everyone laughing even more.

Everyone except Verity, who seemed rather miffed at being overshadowed by her friends. Before she could say anything, Franklin turned to Lisette.

"What about you, Miss Darling? Care to give the comedians at the table a run for their money?"

Lisette had thought of one but certainly didn't want to compete against others. Still, she was feeling caught up in the revelry. She thought of the days when she and her Uncle Avery used to trade jokes and verses that were improper for a fourteen-year-old girl. For the first time in a long time, thinking of him didn't make her morose, remembering the night when everyone in her family had still been alive. Perhaps this party was a sign that it was okay to be that improper girl again.

"Oh, alright," she said, but gave Franklin a teasingly speculative look. "However, if I win, I get to transfer my prize to someone else at the table."

"How altruistic of you. Now, I'm not so sure I want to hear it."

"Come on, Lisette!" Betts encouraged.

Lisette grinned and recited hers:

There once was a dinosaur lassie
Who was very well known to be sassy
With a shake of her tail, she'd make the boys yell
Then give them more jazz than Count Basie

It also didn't *quite* rhyme, but Joann, Franklin, and,

surprisingly, Geoff were the first to erupt with laughter, the first even clapping in appreciation, dropping ash from her cigarette onto the tablecloth. Lennie lifted his champagne to her and chuckled. Betts snorted and tittered and Patti blushed, biting back a smile.

"It's good to meet a young whippersnapper who actually remembers when jazz had an entirely different meaning," Joann said with a cackle.

"I don't get it, and who's Count Basie?" Verity asked, pouting with irritation.

"Never mind that, my dear. Bask in the glory of your youth," Franklin said, which was entirely the wrong thing to say.

"Well..." Verity sniffed. "Since I'm such a *baby*, I get to decide who wins, and I say it's Neville. Congratulations, Nevie!"

The laughter died down. Betts looked fit to kill. Patti was obviously disappointed but shrugged it off. Everyone else stirred in their seats with discomfort. Though Lisette couldn't see him from her vantage point, she was sure Neville was the most uncomfortable one of all.

"Nonsense, Verity. The others were so much better. Let's be fair now," Neville protested.

"I'm the birthday girl, and I get to choose. It's *you*!"

Lennie was the one to start the round of applause, far more robustly than necessary. "Congratulations, old sport!"

Franklin, Hedley, Patti, and Lisette were quick to join him if only to cut through the unease in the air. Cynthia tepidly joined in, her mouth set into a firm line of embarrassment. Joann arched an eyebrow and sucked on her cigarette holder. Troy breathed out a laugh and shook his head in mild wonder, then took a long sip of wine. Betts sulked.

"I suppose the headline goes to you, Neville. Well done. Say, Lennie, care to bring up any *more* interesting news that will earn me an irate phone call from my brother over in New York, wondering what the heck is going on out here?" Franklin asked, mostly in a good-natured way, but Lisette could see how taut his jaw was. Verity, at the other end of the table, looked perfectly pleased with herself. It was going to be a long night.

CHAPTER SEVEN

THE REST of dinner continued in a way that made everyone almost forget about how awkwardly it had started. With that much "comedic wit" at the table, it was inevitable. In fact, the only continuing danger was the fear of someone choking from laughter.

"...an I tells him, honey, you gotta pick, one end or the other, this ain't no see-saw."

Lisette couldn't even bring the spoon of ice cream to her mouth, she was laughing so hard. Joann not only had the best jokes, but she knew how to deliver them in just the right manner, timing, and with a facial expression to hit them out of the park. It helped that there had been several rounds of wine served in addition to those first glasses of champagne. Even Scrooge himself would have been in a merry mood with that much grape juice in his veins.

"Joann, I am humbled by your delightfully devilish mind," Lennie said, laughing as he raised his glass to her.

"If you like my mind, darling, wait'll you see what the rest of me can do."

Lisette gave up, putting the spoon of ice cream down

before it threatened to hit the table instead of her mouth as she laughed. "I think I'm done."

"Me too," Betts said with a pert smile. "I need to watch the figure after all."

Patti silently put her spoon down, wistfully looking at her half-finished bowl. Everyone else did the same.

"Okay, okay, okay!" Verity said, riding the wave of laughter to make another announcement. She stood up, bouncing in place and waving her hands to quiet everyone. "Now that dinner is done, I have a little present for all of you!"

"Garçon!" Her voice was loud enough to have one of the waiters scurrying in.

"Oui, mademoiselle?" The subtle hint of a sardonic smile on his lips made Lisette think he knew that garçon meant "boy." A few people at the table sported smirks. Verity seemed innocently pleased by the use of French.

"It's time for the boxes, *see vou play.*"

He just barely rolled his eyes behind her back at her terrible French, then nodded and left. Everyone at the table looked at one another with curious smiles, wondering what was coming next. Only Franklin had a knowing look on his face as he eyed a giddy Verity from across the table. Waiters came in to clear away their plates and table settings. Once there was nothing left but the candles and the floral display, they returned with black square boxes, each tied with white satin bows. They were about twelve inches square but only five inches high. The waiters seemed to instinctively know which box went to which person. Everyone stared down at their boxes wondering what they might be.

"Well, go ahead—open them!" Verity said with a giggle.

The guests all laughed nervously and opened their boxes. Everyone gingerly pulled out what was in theirs.

Each was a half mask, every one a different animal done only in black and white. They were made quite well, something you'd find at an elegant masquerade ball. Lisette saw that hers was a dove, all white feathers with a black pointed beak just above her exposed mouth.

"Is this a rat?" Betts protested next to her. Lisette looked over to find hers was done in white fur with a small, pointed snout, a black nose on the end, whiskers, and round ears.

"It's a mouse, silly," Verity said with a laugh.

That didn't do much to ease Betts's frown. She craned her neck to see what Patti had. Even still in the box, the long ears indicated it was a white rabbit with a black nose. Lennie had a monkey. Next to Lisette, Franklin pulled out his white lion mask to hold up against his face with a grin. Lisette looked around the table to see what everyone else had. Joann had a white cat, the thick fur reminding Lisette of Isabelle, her own white Persian. Cynthia's was a zebra. Troy got a fox. Even though she couldn't see them, she could tell from the comments of others that Geoff had a wolf, Neville had a raccoon, and Hedley had an owl. Verity's looked like a swan with all-white feathers and a flat black bill.

The guests were ossified enough for the reactions to range from amusing to hilarious to confounding. They brought the masks up to their faces and made corresponding animal noises. Even Betts perked up, realizing she could squeak out a mouse sound in a provocative way.

"Everyone has to call me Minnie Mouse for the rest of the night," she said in a high-pitched falsetto.

"Wait a second, this isn't right. They got the boys' masks all mixed up!" Verity frowned around the table. "Troy should be the raccoon, and—"

"I'm fine being a raccoon," Neville quickly reassured her.

"And I think the wolf is quite fitting for me, at least according to a few of the actors and actresses I have under contract," Geoff said with a guffaw.

"Besides, I think there are more fitting occupants at the table for a raccoon mask than yours truly," Troy said. His drunken smirk Neville's way wasn't lost on Lisette. Raccoons were notorious little pests, usually found rifling around for scraps in trash cans. It was a pathetic and quite mean insult, even for someone as obviously drunk as Troy was.

"It's fine, Verity, everyone is happy with their masks," Franklin said.

Verity pouted for just one more second, a crease of concern as she glanced Troy's way. Then, she shrugged and laughed it off. "I suppose it doesn't matter. The boys can trade if they want to later." Her eyes widened with excitement at the next announcement. "So you're probably wondering what this is all about. Well, we're goin' to have a masquerade party to ring in my birthday!"

As though on cue, the waiters threw black and white confetti into the air. The jazz band picked up the hint and began playing a loud upbeat tune. Everyone laughed and put on their masks. The room was big enough for them to turn the area closest to the band into a dance floor. Betts was smart enough to grab Geoff, urging him out of his seat to dance. Patti and Lennie joined them, the difference in height and his monkey mask creating a comical scene. Troy urged Joann out of her seat and she coquettishly agreed. Neville even managed to get Cynthia up to dance. Hedley danced around the edges in a more dignified manner. Verity escaped for some reason.

"Shall we, Miss Darling?" Franklin asked.

"Only if you call me Lisette."

"Hello, Lisette, I'm Franklin."

She laughed and took his hand to join him in a Charleston.

When Verity returned, she made a show of announcing herself. She had done a wardrobe change into a backless white dress with tiny fluttering sleeves. Around her waist, she wore a wide black ribbon that didn't exactly fit the style, even if it did fit the color theme of the party. With her swan mask, she looked stunningly exotic.

There was no shortage of champagne from that point on. Lisette usually tempered her intake, knowing how quickly those bubbles went to her head. That night, she relaxed enough to enjoy more than usual. Everyone traded partners multiple times, swinging, hopping, shimmying, and making up their own dances, all of it a blur. Some were definitely more ossified than others. Lisette wondered how they would make it to midnight, and worse, what the morning would be like. Hopefully, there was plenty of coffee and Aspirin on board.

The animal masks stayed on. That was mostly due to Verity's insistence on it. Lisette had to admit that it added to the frivolity, and perhaps made people a bit less inhibited. It didn't always present in the best way. Verity was arguing with Lennie at one point, but Lisette couldn't hear what was being said over the sound of the music. She humored Neville making a fool of himself, but fortunately, Geoff had been distracting Cynthia at the time. Both of them were having a surprisingly sedate conversation in a corner. Lisette was close enough to catch snippets of it:

"...both go to Ambrose Westlake. They're in summer classes now..."

"...heard it's a very good school. My grandkids go to..."

"...so expensive. Neville wants to just move back home to Baton Rouge even though he hates..."

"Come join us, Lisette!"

Lisette shifted her attention to Betts and Patti, who were sandwiched on either side of Troy. They took turns pouring champagne down his eagerly open mouth.

Instead, Lennie grabbed her and began an impromptu tango. She was just ossified enough to laugh and play along. His long limbs made it that much more precariously fun. The jazz band was surprisingly versatile, instantly accommodating them with the right music.

At some point, she found herself facing a fox. Troy had his arm tightly around her waist. He could barely stand up and nearly had the both of them toppling over.

"I think maybe you should start taking it easy on the champagne," she said with an uncertain smile. Frankly, the dancing, drinking, and smell of sweat in the air was getting to her.

"Nonsense, sweetie, issa party, ain't it?" He was slurring his words, which meant he most definitely should be limiting his champagne, and anything else.

"Yes, it is, I suppose."

"I know why you invited me, liddle birdie," he mumbled, his attractive mouth curled into a smirk. "You want a part in one of my movies, doncha?"

"I think you have the wrong little birdie," Lisette said with a smile. She still had her mask down, and she could see why he'd mistake her for Verity, especially with that fur on his mask obscuring the view.

"Do I?" He asked, pulling away and regarding her with a frown. He shook his head, more in denial than to clear his mind. "No, no, we directors talk, you know. You're an ambitious little birdie, I'll give you that."

"Again, I'm not that little birdie."

He seemed to find that funny and laughed. "That mask can't hide what you really are, even off the screen, Miss *Verity Vance*."

"Now, I definitely know you have the wrong gal. *Miss Lisette Darling* has never been on the screen, Mr. Turner." She hoped mentioning her name and being more formal would both clear his vision and stop his wandering hands.

"No need to be so formal with me, darlin'. Not someone like you. I know what you are, you little minx. That mask doesn't fool me." He leaned, or more so fell into her, his mouth connecting with her jaw just beneath her ear. She felt a soft laugh against her skin. "Does Frankie-wanky know your secret?"

She tried pushing him away, but it unraveled into something messy. He reached out. Lisette assumed it was to hold onto her to keep from falling, but instead, he jerked her mask up from her face. He stared in drunken surprise, his hand sliding down her cheek and nose, as though wondering if it was real. "By golly, look at you. Such a wonder, so stunning. It really is remarkable."

"Really, Troy!" Lisette protested in anger, slapping his hand away from her face and shoving him off her. "You're getting ridiculous."

Lisette didn't care if she was making a scene, which she most certainly was. The music faltered for a moment, and everyone turned to stare. Particularly when Troy stumbled back and fell to the floor right on his butt. She felt a sense of surreal unease, all those masks staring at her, as though she was some prey caught in a jungle of predators.

"I...I think I just need some fresh air," she said, ripping her mask completely off and storming outside.

The night air hit her face and she breathed it in. It was a relief to have that idiotic mask off her face. Lisette hoped no one would follow her out to make excuses for Troy or ask if she was alright. She just wanted a moment of blessed silence alone. She noted that she was on the side of the boat facing away from the shore. Still, she had the sense they were far enough away that there probably would have been nothing more than barely visible lights in the distance. Something about that made her shiver with unease.

She could hear the muffled sound of Patti and Betts, and perhaps Verity, doing some routine to a spritely song the clarinet was playing. It sounded like they were imitating Bettie Boop. Everyone was laughing and clapping, which was a good sign. Lisette was just glad it was enough to keep them occupied instead of thinking about her and what had just happened with Troy.

She wandered further on until she couldn't hear anything more than the sound of the boat's motor and the ocean breeze. That gave her a view from the other side. It took her a moment to realize what was amiss. When it hit her, she blinked in surprise and dismay.

Where in heaven's name was the shore?

CHAPTER EIGHT

LISETTE WENT ALL the way to the top deck where there was a full panoramic view on all sides of the yacht. It was official, they were so far out to sea that she couldn't even see the shoreline. At night, it should have been easier to spot, as lit up as it would have been. Even if they were along a stretch of shore that was barely inhabited, there should have been at least one or two lights. But it was pitch black all around her. Granted, the moon wasn't doing much of a job providing light, sliver that it was in the sky.

"I suppose it doesn't matter," she told herself. There was an experienced captain at the helm and she knew how to swim. It wasn't as though she was on board the Titanic in the middle of the frozen Atlantic. "Not the best imagery, Lisette."

She tried to shake off her anxiety, but that only made her more disconcerted. Still, the last thing she wanted to do was go back inside just yet. She wasn't quite ready to—

Lisette whipped her head around when she heard someone step foot on the top deck where she stood alone.

"Oh, sorry, ma'am." It was the trumpet player, with a look of stunned apology on his face. He had a cigarette pack already in his hands to shake one out. "I didn't mean to bother you."

Lisette laughed softly with relief and waved off his apology. "First of all, it's 'Lisette.' Second, I don't mind the company."

He studied her with uncertainty, trying to read her signals, then nodded, apparently accepting her at her word. Still, he remained on the other side of the deck. He pulled out a cigarette and held the pack out toward her with a questioning look.

She again waved him off. "I don't smoke. Not really."

"I can go to another part of the boat if you like."

"I don't mind the smoke. Besides, I'd rather have a witness to testify on my behalf if I have to give a certain man a black eye should he try to make his way up here."

He laughed softly and stuck the cigarette in his mouth, then lit it. After taking a drag, he breathed out smoke. "Yeah, I saw that. I was surprised you didn't leave him with a good shiner then and there, to be honest."

"I'm kind of surprised myself," she said with a smile. "Once upon a time, I would have. I should go back to being that Lisette."

He nodded and took another drag, breathing white smoke up into the dark sky. Before taking another puff, he squinted one eye at her. "You sure you don't mind me being up here?"

"To be honest, I feel safer out here all alone with you than I do in there." She grimaced and shot him an apologetic smile. "No offense meant."

"None taken."

They stood in silence for a while, him smoking his cigarette and Lisette feeling her taut and tangled nerves unravel. With the white coat, his skin looked even darker, but Lisette could still see the sharp features of his handsome face. She could understand why Patti had tried flirting with him.

He must have felt her staring at him, because he spoke, still staring up at the smoke he had just breathed out. "Count Basie, huh?"

Lisette laughed, thinking of her limerick. "I actually love jazz."

One brow quirked up and he rolled his eyes to her.

She coughed out an embarrassed laugh. "I mean the music!"

"Mmm-hmm," he hummed.

"Don't look at me that way, I'm no pampered princess." Lisette sassed, pursing her lips.

He laughed. "Pampered princesses are the jazz world's bread and butter. Nothing makes the old man blow his toupee quicker."

Lisette laughed again. "Well, my old man isn't one to put on airs. Going to a jazz club would hardly be my worst offense. As I said, I do actually love jazz."

"Everyone loves jazz," he offered with a shrug.

Lisette gave him an incredulous smile. "I wish I had your self-confidence."

"Skin this color, it's gotta be thick."

Lisette tilted her head in acknowledgment of that. "Touché."

"You been to any clubs in L.A.? I work mostly out at the Satin Club on Crenshaw. I might could get you in some of the nicer ones ahead of the line."

"Isn't the point of going to jazz clubs visiting the not-so-nice ones?"

"Touché," he said, making her laugh.

"Thanks all the same. I may take you up on that. I don't visit them as often as I'd like to. Maybe because I have a rather bad memory associated with one of them."

His expression became serious. "That so?"

"Don't worry, no clubs in Los Angeles. This was back in New York."

"You don't say? I come from back in New York, though my folks are from Mississippi. Which club you talkin' about?"

Lisette squinted one eye at him. "The Peacock Club."

He threw his head back and laughed. "Old Jack Sweeney's place? That joint's too swanky to throw out a gal like you."

"Not if you're only fourteen at the time."

He laughed again and considered her. "Well, well, well. I 'spect if you was to try and sneak into any clubs out here, you wouldn't need old Leroy's help getting in. Mind my asking what happened?"

Lisette became more somber and shook her head. "It'll ruin the party mood."

"I dig," he said nodding, his expression just as, if not more serious. He frowned out to the ocean. "We all got luggage we wish we could leave at the depot."

"I'm ruining the fun, Leroy, was it? Let's focus on something more pleasant. After all, this is meant to be a celebration, no?" She rolled her eyes. Even she could hear the sarcasm in her voice.

He flashed a smile and took a long drag as he brought his attention back to her. "And yet you don't seem to be in a celebratory mood, if you don't mind my sayin' so."

"No, Leroy, I'm not. And I suspect it's only going to get worse as the night continues."

He grinned around his cigarette. "You s'spect so?"

Lisette pondered it for a long moment. "Ever feel like Daniel facing the lions?"

"That bad, huh?"

She sighed. "I suppose it could be worse."

He coughed out a laugh. "You won't find me complaining about free champagne and a paying gig, Miss Lisette."

"Just Lisette," she corrected. "And here's a tip for you, Leroy, free champagne is never free."

He coughed out a laugh. "Ain't that the truth."

"Those masks have only made everyone worse. Even I found myself getting rather uninhibited."

"Isn't that the point of masks? Become somebody you ain't? People like to hide who they truly are. Or maybe it just reflects the real you, deep inside."

"I'm hardly a dove."

"You didn't get to pick your own mask, now did you? Maybe that's just how the birthday girl views you."

"I can see how she considers herself a swan."

"Mmm," he said noncommittally, looking off in thought with a slight frown.

Lisette sighed. "You know what? I think I will take one of those cigarettes. That's what every guilty party gets before facing the firing squad, no?"

"You feeling guilty about something?" He pulled out his cigarette pack and walked over.

"Complaining about free champagne, especially in these trying times?" Lisette offered, making him laugh.

She was just about to select a cigarette when they both

heard a bang. Her hand stopped mid-air and her eyes connected with his.

"Was that—?"

"A gunshot? I s'spect it was."

They both ran back down the stairs.

CHAPTER NINE

HAVING LONGER legs and not hobbled with heeled shoes, Leroy was the first to enter the large room where the party had come to a full stop. Lisette was a few steps behind him, her heart in her throat.

The scene before them was surprisingly still and silent. Everyone seemed to be processing what they were staring at. Their masks were either fully pulled off, or lifted to the tops of their heads. A rabbit mask and a mouse mask lay on the dinner table. Betts and Patti were near the band, hugging each other, their eyes filled with horror. Joann was near the door, her cigarette holder held in mid-air, a thin trail of smoke burning the butt down to ash. Cynthia was curled into Neville's side. Hedley was near the dinner table, her hands still to her ears from the sound of the gunshot. Lennie was in the middle of the dance floor, his long arms held out as though he could keep everyone in place to avoid chaos from erupting. Geoff rushed in from the door leading out on the other side of the room, having heard the gunshot as Lisette and Leroy had.

Everyone was facing one corner where Verity stood over

a man with a fox mask still on his face. He lay on the ground, dead to the world. In her hand was a gun, still smoking from the single shot she'd fired.

Hedley was the first to start screaming.

That was enough to break the spell of frozen silence everyone else seemed to be under. Betts and Patti both added their screams and cries of horror.

"What have you done, Verity?" Geoff breathed out.

"I…" Verity looked down at the still smoking gun in her hands as though surprised it was there.

"What in the hell is going on in here?" Franklin yelled, storming in from wherever he had been, down another hallway. That silenced the loudest of the reactions. His eyes followed the direction everyone else was looking.

Verity turned to Franklin, a look of bewildered shock on her face. "Franklin, I…"

"Don't say a word, Verity," Franklin ordered, rushing over.

That seemed to snap her senses into place. Verity instantly dropped the gun and stepped away from Troy's body, then turned to curl herself into Franklin's open arms.

"Does someone want to tell me what happened in here?" Geoff demanded, looking around with an incredulous expression. "Is Troy dead? Did she shoot him?"

That was exactly what Lisette wanted to know. She looked around, waiting to see who would answer Geoff first. Most of them looked too stunned to speak.

"No one say a word," Franklin said, his chin resting on Verity's head as she began to cry into his chest. He eyed each person in the room, one by one. "This is a criminal matter. We don't want anything interfering with the investigation."

"But—"

"Not a word!" Franklin said, interrupting Patti before she could finish her protest.

"Franklin, we need to deal with this. Troy Turner is lying here dead on your boat, for heaven's sake!" Geoff said.

"Yes, I realize that," he replied in a curt tone. He sighed, suddenly looking irritated at Verity's sobbing which was bordering on hysterical. His eyes rolled to where Patti and Betts were. "Patti, can you take her to her cabin? Maybe get her some whiskey to settle her nerves."

"Is that such a good idea?" Lisette said. "If she has to speak to the police then—"

Verity cried out against Franklin's chest, drowning out anything Lisette might have said to finish that sentence.

"Can't you see she's in no condition to be coherent?" Franklin diverted his attention back to Patti. "Take her, for crying out loud!"

That had Patti flinching, but she quickly scurried over. Franklin detached Verity from himself and swiveled her weak body toward Patti, who struggled to half-escort half-lug the still sobbing Verity down the hallway out of sight.

"You go with them, Bethany."

Betts quickly hurried after them. Only when the sound of her crying disappeared did Franklin speak again. He looked around, his eyes settling on Neville and Cynthia, who was shaking in his arms. "Neville, I need you to speak with the captain. Tell him that someone has died and we need to get the ship back to shore. He should get in touch with the police as well, I suppose."

"I should really stay with—"

"Cynthia will be fine in her room. She looks as though she needs to rest as well."

"I'm not leaving my husband!"

"You'll be fine with us in here until he gets back,"

Franklin said in a soothing voice. "We'll get you some brandy or wine and—"

"I don't want brandy or wine! I want to know why that woman killed Troy!"

"Let's not get hysterical now, Cynthia. We're all still in shock and that might color our sensibilities." His voice was more patronizing than calming now.

Lisette could see it had no effect on her. She clung to Neville even tighter.

"I'll go," Hedley said, the strain in her voice still evident even as she put on a brave show for Franklin's sake.

"Thank you, Hedley," he said, jerking his head in a nod of appreciation.

The way she fled, Lisette wondered if she just wanted to escape the room with Troy's body.

"Now then," he said carefully scanning the room with a grim look. "Everyone here should remain calm and more importantly, levelheaded. I'll say it again, let's try to refrain from babbling about what happened, allowing our coloring of the situation to run wild."

It seemed to Lisette that the situation was quite clear: Verity had shot Troy. She just couldn't figure out why. Where had she even gotten the gun? Did she bring it on board knowing she would need it? Who brings a gun to their own birthday party?

Lisette looked around the room, studying each face to see if she could read the answers there. Leroy had wisely and quietly sidled back to the safety of his fellow members of the jazz band. They were huddled together, no doubt already conspiring their code of silence. Lisette couldn't blame them for maintaining their blinders when it came to pointing the finger at a white woman, especially when that woman was the favorite of one of the wealthiest men in America.

Joann had a surprisingly cool, assessing look on her face as she resumed smoking her cigarette.

Lennie still looked struck, as though he couldn't believe what had happened. There was a small crease of consternation in his brow. Lisette had read his feelings for Verity all day, so it was no surprise he would be distraught.

Cynthia still looked on the verge of hysterics and Neville seemed more concerned with keeping her afloat than anything. He held on tightly, staring blankly at a wall as she shook in his arms.

Geoff just looked irate. "Now see here, Franklin, you may be fine wandering in the dark, but I want to know what the hell happened. We aren't talking about some party mishap, this is *murder*!"

"That's for the police to determine. At any rate, there's no threat now. The gun is on the floor, which is exactly where it should remain. In fact, that is all the more reason we all ought to leave this room as it may be a crime scene. Short of going outside to the upper deck, there is no room large enough to hold us all, so I have to insist everyone retire to their cabins until we reach the shore and the police can talk with each of you individually."

That was a sound argument to which no one could offer a protest. Frankly, Lisette would have rather gone back outside for some fresh air. She couldn't imagine being in that cramped cabin waiting for them to get back to land. She still had no idea just how far offshore they were.

One by one, they all left, like mute sheep. The band, needing no further urging, took their instruments and escaped to wherever their quarters for the trip were located. Lisette and Geoff were the last to remain in the room.

"Ah...Miss Darling. I can see you are upset."

"Not upset, just wondering what happened."

"I beg your pardon? You weren't here?"

"No. Whose gun is that?" Lisette jerked her chin toward the weapon still on the floor.

"That's irrelevant. I think you should do as everyone else has done and go to your—"

"How far offshore are we?"

"What?"

"I was on the top deck and noticed I couldn't see the lights of the shoreline. How far out to sea are we?"

"I...what does that have to do with anything?"

It occurred to Lisette that it might have a lot to do with plenty. If they were in international waters then that made things sticky. She wasn't quite sure, but she thought that meant jurisdiction would be in the hands of whatever country the ship was registered in. At the moment, Franklin had a point, it had nothing to do with anything. Not anything pressing, at any rate.

"You said you were just outside?"

"Yes."

"So, you didn't actually see what happened?" Franklin studied her carefully.

Lisette returned a level gaze. "No, that's why I'm asking these questions."

"Ah," he said, nodding, "I can understand why you would be particularly dismayed."

"That's a bit of an understatement. Troy Turner is dead, not even cold yet on the floor right in front of us."

"Yes, it is upsetting." That paternalistic tinge in his voice grated on her nerves. "But the point remains, this room may be the scene of the crime, so I have to ask you to leave and return to your cabin. If you need a sedative, I believe Verity has some."

"No, I'm fine, thank you," Lisette gritted out. She took a second to alter her voice into something more simpering. "How long do you think it will be until we get to shore?"

"To make it back to the marina, it should be a few hours at most," he said with an avuncular smile meant to reassure her.

It did nothing but make her suspicious. A few hours was plenty of time for memories to play tricks, stories to change, ideas to form....and conspiracies to develop. Perhaps even for bodies to disappear.

Lisette wasn't so cynical she thought Franklin would be bold enough to throw Troy's body overboard. But that odd sense she had, which had served her well in her profession as a fixer, was tingling in her head telling her something was playing out even as she returned to her cabin. Perhaps her priority should be keeping herself from becoming the next victim.

CHAPTER TEN

LISETTE REMAINED in her empty cabin alone until they reached the shore. The first part of that time had been spent recovering from the shock of Troy Turner's murder. It was an odd and upsetting feeling, someone murdered only moments after personally interacting with them, no matter how unpleasant that interaction had been.

But Troy was dead all the same. There had been enough people in that room to point the finger at the suspect, which most certainly had to be Verity. At least Troy would have that bit of justice.

Still...

It hadn't slipped past Lisette that Franklin had been awfully quick to send everyone to their rooms and keep them from talking to one another. She also felt that sending Betts to join Patti and Verity was a subtle manipulation that kept either of them from being in the same cabin with Lisette.

As such, Lisette was still in the dark about what had led to Verity shooting Troy. That part at least she was certain of —though she obviously couldn't testify to it under oath.

After well over an hour of her mind working like a piston, even that she wasn't certain of. She hadn't even thought to change out of her evening dress.

When a horn sounded, alerting them that they were close to the dock again, she looked through the tiny port hole. She breathed out some of her tension when she saw the marina, or at least the lights indicating it was close. It would be a few hours before the sun gave even a hint of rising in the east, so everything, save for the lights of the shore, was still dark.

Lisette saw no reason to remain in her cabin at that point. As she opened the door to leave, she wondered why she had stayed there like an obedient child for so long. She walked down the narrow hallway and made her way up to the top deck, avoiding the room where Troy's body presumably still remained.

When she arrived, she saw that she wasn't the only one who had the same idea. Joann leaned against the railing with a glass of something from the unmanned bar in one hand and her cigarette holder in the other.

She offered Lisette a placid smile. "Had enough of brewing in your cabin? Me, I was about ready to go mad."

"The police will want to speak to you when we get ashore." She eyed the glass in Joann's hand.

Joann laughed. "Honey, this is the lubrication my mouth needs to get going."

"Otherwise you wouldn't talk?" Lisette was puzzled.

"Otherwise, I might do something stupid, like—" Joann stopped, offered Lisette another tepid smile, then finished off her drink.

"What *did* happen last night?"

Joann smirked, threw the glass overboard, and then

wagged her finger at Lisette. "Uh-uh-uh, Miss Darling. You know the rule, no talky-talky."

Lisette cooled her gaze. "Because Franklin said so?"

"Because loose lips in this business are dangerous. So are curious ears."

"I'm not too worried about my ears."

"A shame, they're as pretty as the rest of you." Joann turned her head to face the looming shore. "The only thing I can tell you is Verity Vance is either going down for murder...or she'll be the biggest star this town has ever seen."

———

The police had been waiting when the yacht finally docked. Two agents from the FBI were also there. Lisette could only assume the captain wasn't sure when and where the murder had happened and thus couldn't give a definitive answer as to whether they were in international waters, or within the three-mile mark of California waters.

Both parties seemed eager to take control of the case until it was sussed out. As such, each person in attendance was to be questioned by both a member of the LAPD and the FBI at the same time.

They hadn't been alone in their arrival. The press had already caught wind of the story, such as it was. All they probably knew was that someone had died, most likely murdered, which was enough to have their tails wagging, cameras already set up to snap. Pretty girls, wealthy moguls, and Hollywood celebrities were media gold.

Perhaps that was why Verity had been held in custody in her cabin, supervised by two policemen. If she was smart, and Lisette had a pretty good idea she was, she wasn't saying a word.

No one else had been permitted to leave the boat or remain in their room. The authorities corralled the passengers to the upper deck, including the jazz band, as most of them had been witnesses to the shooting. Up top, they were left with two policemen to supervise them, making sure they didn't talk to one another or nip something from the bar. The crew was rounded up somewhere else.

Lisette eyed her fellow passengers. It was now late enough that the brightened sky provided light, even if the sun had yet to pierce the horizon. In the dull, lavender dawn she noticed how nervous they all seemed. Perhaps it was the police presence suddenly waking them up to the realization that a serious crime had been committed.

One by one, they had each been taken somewhere below to be interviewed. When they returned, they either looked pale and sick or nervous. Presumably, this was the first time most of them had been in such a situation, so it was understandable they'd be rattled. All the more so when faced with members of two different government organizations.

Lisette had made it clear she hadn't been in the room at the time of the shooting, which was presumably why she was last to be selected for an interview, save for the band members. When it was finally her turn, she was escorted down to a suite that housed a desk and several chairs. It must have been Franklin's cabin, commandeered for the interviews.

All three men wore suits and ties. Lisette could easily identify the g-men, as they were called in most gangster films, because their suits were darker and more uniform in how they looked. L.A. detectives were given a more general "professional" dress code. The member of the LAPD had on a brown suit.

"Good morning," one of the federal men said. "I'm Agent Downing and this is my partner Agent Bernback. We're with the Federal Bureau of Investigation."

"And I'm Detective Grant with the Los Angeles Police Department," the third man hastily added, his jaw tightening ever so slightly.

"The FBI?" Lisette asked, her eyes wide with wonder in the way she knew would make her seem naïve. "Why ever are you involved?"

The three men glanced at one another before Agent Downing answered. He offered a reassuring smile and spoke in a voice reserved for pretty little women who were easily distressed. "There's some issue as to exactly when and where the shooting took place, which brings into question jurisdictional matters. Nothing you have to worry about. Consider us as no different from Detective Grant here. We're police, just as he is, only federal."

Detective Grant seemed to take that as a slight and glowered ever so slightly. Having once been involved with a detective from the LAPD for several months, Lisette knew that they usually had no problem allowing the feds to step in and take over a case. They had more resources and any help was welcome. All the better to allow them to take the heat if things went downhill. However, a case that was both so high profile and seemingly open-and-shut was like finding a goose with a golden egg. Yes, they would have a fine time battling it out over this one.

"That's odd, I was almost certain we were more than three miles from shore. I didn't see any lights from land."

That perked them up. After looking at one another again, Agent Downing spoke up. "It seems you were traveling along a stretch of the California Coast that is mostly unpopulated. Also, there was a marine layer that would have blocked visibility. Whether or not the ship was in international waters at the time of the, ah, incident is in dispute."

"I see." What Lisette really saw was that it was rather convenient that the captain had been traveling right along the three-mile mark the entire time they'd been at sea. Not so convenient for the authorities.

"Now then, I understand you were not in the room when the shot went off?"

"No, but I heard it."

"Yes. Where were you, exactly?"

"On the upper deck, getting some fresh air."

"And were you alone?"

"Until the trumpet player from the band, Leroy, came up for a cigarette. I didn't get his last name."

They all stared at her for a moment, and she could practically read the tawdry thoughts running through their minds. Their frowns of disapproval all but read it to her, word for word.

"Is that illegal?"

Agent Bernback coughed.

"Of course not," Agent Downing said with a pat smile. "Let's continue."

And so it continued. After giving her basic information, they proceeded with their questions. No, she hadn't seen Verity fight with Troy. No, she couldn't think of a reason why she might have wanted to shoot him. No, she had no idea why he'd been invited or how they had known each other previously. In fact, she was rather ignorant about anything concerning the shooting.

"How do you know Verity Vance, Miss Darling?"

"I don't. Not personally, at any rate."

There was a pause of confusion before Agent Downing continued. "So, you know Franklin Winthorpe?"

"I'm familiar with him, and I've met him before, but I wouldn't consider us friends or associates." She continued, answering the question they were really asking. "If you want to know why I was invited this weekend, I have no idea."

They all studied her with suspicion.

"So, you received an invitation from someone you don't know and—"

"I know *who* they are, of course. I work at Olympus Studios. Though, Verity isn't exactly Carole Lombard. Honestly, before she, ah, *connected* with Franklin Winthorpe, I wouldn't have even known her name. Hollywood is filled with hundreds if not thousands of beautiful women serving as extras in the hopes of being discovered. I couldn't possibly know them all. It seems Verity finally was discovered, in a way."

"You didn't find it suspicious that you were sent an invitation, given that you have no prior close relationship with the two people hosting this trip?"

"Of course I did."

"Yet, you came anyway?"

"Would you have turned it down?" She arched an eyebrow questioningly.

Detective Grant smirked. The two agents maintained their poker faces.

"I've noticed that you look very similar to Miss Vance."

"Even your dresses are alike," Agent Bernbach noted.

"That thought hadn't eluded me," she said dryly. "But my birthday is in November and I shall be turning twenty-five, not twenty-one. As for the dress, it was a black and white themed weekend. Naturally, there would be some similarities when it came to formal wear. There was a fifty-fifty chance either of us would either be in black or white."

That idea sparked a troubling notion in Lisette's head. Verity had changed into her long white dress with a black ribbon belt after the masks came out. Very similar to Lisette's with a black sash. Even their masks were similar, both with white feathers and black beaks.

"Is there something on your mind, Miss Darling?"

Lisette snapped back to the present, focusing her attention on Agent Downing. "Not at all."

He studied her for a moment, no doubt as some tactic to get her talking. When she didn't bite, he continued. "How did you know Troy Turner?"

"I didn't, not personally. Olympus Studios has worked with him as a director before, so in that capacity, I have some connection to him. However, there is no personal connection."

"Is there anyone on board that you have a personal connection with?"

"Not really. Almost everyone I know simply from working in the film industry."

"Not even members of the band?" Agent Bernbach asked, unable to hide the slightly leering look. "I know a lot of young women enjoy going to those sorts of clubs. Slumming it, they call it."

"I would neither call it 'slumming,' nor would I deny going. I enjoy jazz music, but no, I don't know these particular jazz players personally. Or biblically. That *is* what you're asking, isn't it?"

The frown his partner gave him had him abashed, which gave Lisette some satisfaction. Even Detective Grant looked amused.

"We're not here to delve into your," Agent Downing cleared his throat before saying, "biblical relationships, Miss Darling. Unless, of course, you know anyone on board in that manner?"

"No."

"Well then." He cleared his throat again. "I understand everyone was wearing masks at the time of the shooting?"

"I had taken mine off when I went up to get some air."

"And your mask, what was it?"

"A dove, at least I assume so. All white with feathers."

"All white? No black?"

"Except for the beak, but again, I had taken mine off when I left."

"And you left solely to get some fresh air?"

"Yes."

"Not to get away from Troy Turner?"

"I beg your pardon?"

"Several people claimed you and Mr. Turner had some kind of altercation prior to your leaving."

"Did they?" Lisette's voice was testy, making her sound defensive. She normalized it before continuing. "He was drunk and overly flirtatious. Certainly nothing worth killing over."

"Of course not." The pat smile was back. "What exactly did he say to you during this altercation."

"I take issue with the term 'altercation.' It was at most nothing more than unwanted attention. As for what he said, he thought I was Verity."

"How do you know?"

"Because he said something about me inviting him because I wanted a part in his film."

"Was that all he said?"

Lisette sighed. "He also said something about my

—*her* keeping a secret, and asked whether Franky—whether *Franklin* knew." She wasn't about to repeat the term "Frankie-wanky" to these men.

All three men blinked with renewed interest.

"And what secret would that be?"

"I have no idea," Lisette said with exasperation. "In his drunken state, he thought I was Verity Vance, just as you three alluded to a moment ago. Perhaps you should be asking her what secrets she has that Troy might know."

"Thank you for that suggestion, Miss Darling. Was there anything else he said?"

"Nothing sensical. He said 'I know what you are, you little minx.' That I couldn't hide behind my mask. Then he pulled mine up and began pawing at my face telling me... basically that I was attractive." Lisette hated touting her beauty and knew it might come off as boastful if she repeated everything he'd said word for word.

"And you're certain he was still mistaking you for Miss Vance?"

"He seemed surprised when he pulled up my mask. Besides, as I said, his prior comments certainly didn't apply to me. Troy knows enough about me to know I'm no actress."

"What were his exact words during that final exchange?"

Lisette sighed. "'By golly, look at you.' Then, something about me being a wonder and stunning. 'It's remarkable,' or something like that. I don't remember, I was simply trying to get away."

The three men studied her in a way she didn't like. Then, Agent Downing cleared his throat and sat up straighter before continuing.

"Now, I'd like you to go over the events of the day as you

remember up until you, as you say, heard the gunshot, and everything that occurred after that. Specifically, anything that might have involved the deceased, Troy Turner, and Verity Vance."

Lisette did, as succinctly as possible. They had a chuckle over the limericks, though Agent Bernbach did raise an eyebrow at her usage of jazz.

"So, no, I didn't actually see the shooting take place, but when I returned to the room, Verity was standing in one corner over his body with the gun in her hand." She gave them all an assessing look. "Surely at least a few of the others saw the shooting take place?"

The uncomfortable and disgruntled looks on their faces astounded her. "Haven't they?" Lisette demanded.

"Let's go back to the shooting," Agent Downing said. "You said you came back into the room and Verity was holding the gun. After that, a few people started screaming, then she dropped the gun?"

"Yes."

"Did you see anyone pick it up?"

"No, Franklin rightfully declared that it was a crime scene and we all needed to leave. The last I saw, it was right where Verity had dropped it."

"So you didn't return to the room after going to your cabin?"

"No." Lisette eyed the three of them in turn, realizing there was an underlying question they weren't asking. "Why?"

Agent Downing ignored her query. "Thank you for your time and for answering our questions, Miss Darling. We have your contact information here and we will be in touch should we need anything else from you." His smile was essentially a dismissal. But he left her with a warning.

"As this is still an open investigation, you are strictly forbidden from speaking to anyone, particularly the press about what happened here. We still have to notify Mr. Turner's next of kin and we'd hate for them to find out via the morning news instead of from us."

"Of course."

"That will be all, thank you."

Lisette studied all of them a moment longer before realizing she wasn't getting any more information, so she stood and slowly left. When she returned to the upper deck, all the other passengers turned their heads to study her. She could tell they had the same itch to ask what she had said as she did for them. Lisette had the distinct feeling that not a single one of them had confessed to seeing Verity pull the trigger.

CHAPTER ELEVEN

LISETTE HAD BEEN DRIVEN home courtesy of the LAPD. Both the FBI and LAPD had determined the entire yacht a crime scene and forbade anyone from taking anything more than their house or apartment keys and some money. They had all been assured they'd be able to collect their things by the end of the day once everything had been "investigated and processed." That confirmed a sneaking suspicion Lisette had—they still hadn't found the gun.

The big question was, who had taken the gun and what had they done with it?

The drive back to her apartment had given Lisette time to push aside the matter of Verity's guilt and focus on the fact that Troy Turner was dead. It wasn't her first experience with death, or even murder, but it was always a sad affair. Toward the end of the evening, he'd certainly not been a gentleman, but Lisette hardly wished him dead.

She braced herself before entering the apartment. Her roommate and best friend Darcy Pembry would no doubt have questions about her early return home. Lisette doubted the tabloid presses Darcy was so fond of, along with every woman's magazine she could get her hands on, had been quick enough to publish news of a murder on board. And Darcy did love a bit of Hollywood gossip.

Darcy was lying on the sofa in their tiny living room with a sleeping mask on her face. Lisette's white-haired Persian cat, Isabelle de Merteuil, was taking advantage of her prone state, using her stomach as a cat bed.

"Lisette, is that you?" Darcy asked, even though Lisette had quietly entered, assuming she was still asleep. Darcy pulled the mask up and squinted one eye Lisette's way. "Don't tell me the party ended early."

"It did."

Darcy sat up, earning a mewl of protest from Izzy who jumped to the floor and scurried off to her real cat bed in a huff.

"Tell me everything! Particularly, what you had to eat. I decided to punish myself while you were galavanting around the Pacific by doing this apple cider fast for the weekend. You're only allowed two tablespoons of apple cider mixed with eight ounces of water. It's supposed to cleanse the gut and give you healthy glowing skin."

"I swear these helpful little ideas you get from your magazines are going to kill you one day, Darcy." Lisette instantly regretted her choice of words and grimaced.

"Wait, where is your suitcase?"

"That...is a long story."

"Did it fall overboard?" Darcy's dark eyes were wide with surprise. Lisette figured they would grow even wider when she revealed what had really happened. She walked over and sat on the couch next to her.

"No, but the police wouldn't let me take it." Lisette

figured she might as well be the first to tell her everything. Despite the agent's warning, the news was already half-way to the presses as she spoke. She almost laughed at the way Darcy reacted to the mention of "police."

"*Police?* What happened? Was it secretly a gambling operation? Was Franklin smuggling liquor? Oh no wait, that's legal now. Was it an opium den?"

As fun as it was hearing Darcy's wild guesses, Lisette felt the gravity of the situation warranted that she guide the conversation in the direction of the murder.

"Troy Turner was shot, murdered."

"No!" Darcy shot up from the couch and stared at Lisette. Her eyes were indeed much wider than before. "Who killed him?"

"I'm ninety-nine percent certain it was Verity Vance."

"Verity?" Darcy gasped, half filled with excitement and half filled with horror and surprise at the circumstances. Her brow instantly wrinkled into a V. "Wait, did you say ninety-nine percent certain?"

"I wasn't in the room when he was shot. But everything leads me to believe it was her. She was standing right over his body with the gun in her hands. Even one of the other passengers who was presumably there when it happened claimed it was her."

"Jeepers!" Darcy said, falling back onto the couch next to her in shock. She stared ahead at the wall for a moment, absorbing the enormity of the news. She got over it quickly enough to turn to Lisette, her eyes swimming with curiosity. "Tell me everything!"

"I'm not sure how much I should say, seeing as this is a murder investigation. I can tell you about the games and what people wore, a bit about the masks."

"Oh blather about that banana oil. Who cares about— wait, there were masks? What did they look like? Was her dress positively divine? Was she wearing the mask when she shot him?!"

"Darcy."

"What? Lisette, you can't just drop a bomb like that in my lap and expect me to wait the proper amount of time for it to go off. Were they secretly lovers? Franklin Winthorpe must have had a bee in his pants over that one."

"Isn't the phrase bee in his bonnet?"

"Men don't wear bonnets, Lisette, and stop changing the subject."

"Well her dress was very nice. Kind of like the one I'm wearing now." Lisette looked down at the white silk dress, once again pondering the similarities between it and the one Verity had changed into.

Had Verity brought a number of gowns hoping one of them would be similar enough to Lisette's to make it difficult to distinguish between them? Bethany had mentioned something about her bringing a lot of luggage. What if she hadn't been exaggerating? If one limited the color options guests were allowed to wear, that made it easier to guess ahead of time what one woman in particular might wear. Most formal dresses were either white or black, not necessarily a mix of the two. The only tricky part would be style, fabric, and fit. Perhaps someone had told Verity that Lisette often wore the latest in fashion because of her connection to the costuming department at Olympus. That would have further narrowed the options down to modern styles. Out with the oversized winged sleeves, in with slimmer silhouettes.

"You know what, Darcy? I think I truly was set up with that invitation."

"What do you mean?"

Lisette turned to her friend. "I'm almost certain this shooting was pre-meditated, long before the boat even left the dock."

CHAPTER TWELVE

LISETTE HAD DEFLECTED most of Darcy's pressing questions about the murder by detailing what everyone wore, ate, and drank. She had been particularly interested in the Black & White Swans, enough to want to break her fast and try one. Lisette had to bring her back from that ledge by pointing out the poor dear hadn't eaten for almost a day and a half. She added that the poppyseeds didn't add anything ritzy to the drink, they were just an irritating feature to make the drinks at least somewhat black and stay on theme.

After succumbing to sleep for a few hours, Lisette returned to the marina, early enough to beat the others in their return to the yacht. She was hoping to catch a certain passenger returning to get their belongings. It was hard to find a place where she wouldn't be noticed, as the media presence was, if anything, even greater now that the news of a murder had spread.

"Perfect," Lisette whispered to herself when she saw two people in particular arrive together. She waited until they were on the yacht before quickly walking to the boat.

That meant getting past the throng of reporters being held back by a police officer.

"I'm Lisette Darling, here to get my things from the boat," she informed him.

The name was familiar enough to at least a few locals she recognized. Her job was working for the man who fixed public relations disasters for anyone tied to Olympus Studios, which meant she constantly interacted with the press.

"*Lisette!*"

"*Miss Darling!*"

"*Were you on board when the murder occurred? Who was the victim?*"

"*Care to give a statement about what happened?*"

She ignored all of it as the policeman let her through, barking at all of them to remain firmly behind the rope that had been set up to keep them at bay.

She thanked him and quickly headed to the yacht. The policeman guarding it recognized her and let her on without a word. She made her way down to the cabins, where the one she'd shared with Bethany and Patricia—mentally she decided to use their Christian names as a reminder of the seriousness of the situation—was located.

They were both there, quickly packing up their things. They jumped in surprise when Lisette entered the room.

"Well, what a coincidence we're all back at the same time," she said brightly.

Bethany narrowed her eyes with suspicion. Patricia stared, wide-eyed with a nervous expression.

"There certainly are a lot of coincidences, it seems," Lisette continued as she walked over to her cot. Her suitcase had been rifled through, though she couldn't imagine what evidence the police hoped to have found there. She certainly hoped someone hadn't decided to store the missing gun there. She checked it while she repacked her things, just in case.

"Like the coincidence of Verity changing into a gown that looked almost like mine last night," Lisette continued.

They didn't say a word, but Lisette could hear them gathering their things with more urgency behind her. She suspected she only had a minute at most before they left.

"Also, Verity and I look so much alike, don't you think? I half expected her to ask if I would be willing to play her double on a future film."

"Why don't you just ask what you really want to ask?" Bethany said in an exasperated tone.

Lisette stopped packing and turned around to face them. Bethany stared back, the suspicion now fully formed on her face. Patricia stared with uncertainty.

"Alright then, what did you two see last night? Surely one of you must have seen Verity shoot Troy."

They both looked at one another.

"I—"

"We didn't see anything," Bethany said, interrupting Patricia before she could speak. She turned to her friend. "We were both too busy doing that Betty Boop routine, right?"

Lisette waited for Patricia to confirm, but all she did was shrug noncommittally. That was enough for Bethany, who turned back to Lisette with a satisfied smile.

"Let me guess, everyone else was so consumed by your performance that they also didn't see her shoot Troy?"

"I assume so," Bethany said with a shrug. "Besides, with all those masks on, who could have seen anything?"

"You were wearing your masks to perform?"

"Yes."

"Which is odd, because both of yours were on the table by the time I returned."

The first trickle of uncertainty colored Bethany's eyes. "Obviously we took them off amid all the chaos that ensued after the shooting."

"It took me less than twenty seconds to get back into the room. You're telling me that in between the gun going off and my arrival, you removed your masks, walked all the way over to the table to set them down, then returned to where you'd been performing your impression of a cartoon?"

"We didn't see anything, okay?" Bethany said, getting angry. "We already told the police as much when we spoke to them."

"What did Verity tell you while you were supposedly consoling her after she shot Troy?"

"We were busy consoling her, you see?" Bethany's voice was filled with sardonic contempt. "And who says she shot Troy?"

Lisette tried another tactic. "Troy said something to me about a secret while I was dancing with him. You also said something about Verity's past. Is that why she killed him? He learned something about her this weekend? Why did she invite him in the first place?"

Through her parade of questions, Bethany remained impenetrable, a firm set to her mouth indicating she wouldn't be answering any of them. But Lisette had also observed Patricia, who looked ready to burst.

"Patti? Do you know?"

"I..." She turned to Bethany, who had a stare hard enough to cut glass. She turned back to Lisette with a rueful look. "She invited him because she had this plan to star in a film that Neville wanted to produce. It's a comedy, and she does so much better in comedies. She's really funny when you get to know her, always making kooky faces and doing silly little dances. Even Lennie says so. That's why she invited Joann too, to help polish up the script. Troy is the best with comedies so it all made sense. Who woulda thought—"

"Exactly," Bethany said, once again interrupting her. "So why would she kill him?"

"You tell me."

"We didn't see anything," Patricia finally said, though anyone could read the fragile foundation on which her words stood.

"Fine, perhaps you saw how much Verity resembles me. And how alike our masks were?"

"Quit your bag, hers was obviously a swan, and yours a white pigeon." Bethany sneered with amusement.

Lisette ignored that. "I suppose. Though, from the side and back they looked awfully alike, just as Verity and I do."

"But you're older, no?" Bethany seemed to enjoy pointing out that difference.

"And wiser. Wise enough to see a set-up when it's right in front of me." Lisette felt her anger rising. "Anyone else might think that's exactly what was going on. Did she plan Troy's murder beforehand, using me as some patsy to take the fall?"

"Of course not," Patricia protested, looking shocked. She turned to Bethany. "Would she?"

"No, she wouldn't," Bethany snapped, then turned back to Lisette with her hand settled on one hip.

"Did either of you move the gun after the fact?"

"What?" Patricia was genuinely shocked at the question.

Bethany twisted her mouth and glared. "What are you trying to imply? That we interfered after the fact?"

"Did you?"

"Listen lady, it's been swell gettin' to know ya this week-end. A shame it had to end the way it did. But Patticakes and me, we didn't see nothin' or move nothin'. Yous ain't the police and we's ain't gotta say nothin' more to ya. Now we's gonna get outta your way here and leave yous to your packin'." The accent was heavy now, full-fledged New York, probably the Bronx.

It was meant to be intimidating. Betts probably read "money" all over Lisette from the way she talked and carried herself, but her father had deliberately raised her in Queens, so she knew a thing or two about intimidation. "You might wanna think about coverin' for your friend or takin' the fall for her. I suspect the murder wasn't an accident. Who says yous wouldn't be next?"

Yes. she had laid it on a bit thick. It was certainly much more of an accent than she'd ever sported while living in New York—her mother would have had a heart attack if she'd spoken like that in her presence—but it had an impact.

A slow smile spread one side of Bethany's mouth. She tilted her head. "You almost sound authentic. But don't ever think you know anything about me, honey. Betts looks after Betts."

Lisette watched Bethany leave. Patricia gave her one last parting look of apology before she followed Bethany out. She stared at the open door after them, wondering what the heck was going on. The day before, Bethany had been more than happy to make snide remarks about Verity, all but inviting the questions wanting to know more about her past. Now, she was her biggest defender. What had changed in the hours in between?

"Franklin," Lisette hissed to herself. While she'd been isolated in her room, he'd been making the rounds of the passengers on the yacht, promising them the world. Enough so that when they finally arrived to shore, they all suddenly had foggy memories when it came to the shooting.

But the authorities had a body on their hands all the same, and someone was going to have to take the fall.

CHAPTER THIRTEEN

"I THINK I'm in trouble, Herbie."

"And before my morning coffee. It must be serious." He walked through Lisette's small outer office into his larger one located on the lot for Olympus Studios. She followed him in.

The pleasant tone of his voice irritated her. "This is serious, Herbie."

"I take it this is regarding Hedley's article this morning? About a certain director, who shall not be named, who sadly passed away this weekend aboard Mr. Winthorpe's magnificent yachting vessel? I came, I saw, I conquered—a rather fitting appellation, I suppose."

It didn't surprise her that he knew who had died. It would have been impossible to keep that secret for long, and Herbie made a point of knowing everything worth knowing in Hollywood. And this was most certainly worth knowing.

Lisette fell into the seat across from him as he casually took his. He made a point of getting comfortable, his self-described "cuddly" body wriggling until it found just the right position. He sighed with satisfaction, then leaned over, tenting his hands in front of him as he finally focused on Lisette.

"Let me start off by saying that, yes, I am a practicing attorney, licensed right here in the great State of California. As such, anything you say to me is privileged."

"I didn't kill him, Herbie!" Lisette said, incredulous that he would even think such a thing.

"If you did, I can certainly help you. It wouldn't be my first murder case, though I have to confess, I'm a bit rusty on that particular charge."

"I *didn't* kill him!"

He put his hands up, relenting. "Alright then, so what seems to be the trouble?"

"I may be *accused* of killing him."

He studied her for a moment, his lower lip protruding in thought. "I see..."

It was quite clear that he didn't see.

"I wasn't anywhere near him when he was shot. That may very well be the thing that has me going down for it."

His brow wrinkled in confusion. "Perhaps you'd better explain that one to me, Lisette."

Knowing what a good listener he was, Lisette told him everything from the point of boarding the boat and getting Verity's cocktail creation (to which he grimaced) to her discussion with Bethany and Patricia when she returned to get her things. He remained in his prayer-like state, hands tented against his chin, for a long minute afterward. Lisette waited, knowing whatever would eventually come from his lips would be sage advice.

"It's quite obvious that there are forces at work trying to cleanse the slate of guilt, at least as applied to Verity. And by forces, I do mean Franklin Winthorpe. As powerful as I'm sure Miss Vance's charms are, I doubt they have the ammunition to suborn perjury. Winthorpe Media, however, has quite the arsenal. Even this business concerning jurisdiction. Did he deliberately have the captain travel back and forth across the three-mile line?"

"And me, do you think I'm being set up to take the fall?"

He gave her a rueful smile which told her as much. "Obviously, I won't let that happen. The good news is, I don't think it's anything personal. You just happen to look very much like Verity Vance. It's also rather morally problematic. Franklin may be able to persuade people to forget what they saw, but when it comes to an innocent person going to prison, that may be a line too far."

"I feel so reassured."

The sarcasm in her voice wasn't lost on Herbie. "Now, now, no need for that. Your fate isn't yet set in stone. You do have a witness when it comes down to it, though you had to pick the worst possible candidate, I fear."

"I didn't pick him, and frankly I'm grateful to have him, should it come down to it."

"All the same, I don't envy him having to take the stand against Verity Vance. I'm already picturing how that will go down. California likes to think itself above the more, ah, let's just say, stubbornly-minded citizens of this country, but people become awfully regressive when forced to confront certain things face-to-face."

"Again, I feel so reassured."

"Allow me to remind you that there is, as yet, nothing to worry about, at least as far as you're concerned." He held his hands up to stop another protest. "Yes, I know what you're going to say. You and I are in the business of putting out fires before the first spark if we can help it, and this is most definitely a spark. That said, there is one thing that most decidedly separates you and Miss Vance, other than her presumably having pulled the trigger."

"What's that?"

"Motive."

"That's the thing. I don't *know* what her motive is."

"Well then, Miss Darling, it seems you have some work to get to, don't you? I officially relieve you of your duties for Olympus for the day, long enough to find that motive. Learn what her secret is. Yes, it means more work for me, but I'd rather have a bit extra on my plate now than for an indefinite period should you end up in prison."

"Golly, Herbie, I feel so loved and respected."

He laughed. "Off you go now, chop-chop. As you can see from that morning paper, Franklin has his little bees buzzing even as we speak." He gave her an assessing look. "I would suggest incorporating the help of an expert. Two heads are better than one."

"A certain private investigator, by chance?" Lisette twisted her lips.

"One who happens to be quite good at what he does, and also happens to have a soft spot for you, my dear. Perhaps he'll give you a discount. But if it gets the job done, I'll pay him double out of my own pocket."

"That seems rather unseemly."

"More unseemly than prison? A very public and tawdry trial?"

"Point duly noted."

Lisette stood outside the offices of Private Investigator, Byron Linley. She stared at the official gold lettering on the glass door inside the four-story building situated near the heart of downtown Los Angeles. It was smart to have the office there, located in a building with any number of other businesses—dentists, accountants, attorneys, etc.—such that no one would look suspicious entering the building from the street.

"He really must be doing well," she said to herself. When she'd first met him, he hadn't even had an office yet. Now, he had one with a waiting room—and a secretary. Lisette caught a glimpse of her before taking two steps back so she was out of view.

His secretary was a matronly type, the kind who was probably efficient at handling secretarial duties after years of running her home just as efficiently. At least she wasn't young and pretty. Not that it mattered, of course. Lisette had only gone out with Byron once, and even that was for root beers on the Santa Monica Pier. Admittedly one of her most enjoyable dates, though she wasn't quite sure she would label it as such. She had left the status of what they "officially" were up in the air.

Perhaps her concern about what his secretary looked like was telling her what she already knew. Yes, she was most definitely interested in something more than just casual root beers on the pier. But Lisette's history of dating men and finding some reason to end things led her to be cautionary. Besides, she fully intended to head a studio one day, and marriage and children most certainly hampered that. Men could certainly get away with it. She doubted a woman would be afforded the same grace. With that firm thought in her head, she opened the door to enter.

"Good morning," his secretary said, a professionally polite smile on her face. "Do you have an appointment?"

He was already taking appointments?

"Well, um, no. I just need to speak to Byro—Mr. Linley.

My name is Lisette Darling, he should know me. I'd...like to hire his services."

There was no one waiting at the moment so, she nodded and gestured toward a chair. "Of course, if you'll just have a seat while I see if he has a moment."

Lisette took a seat, noting how rigid her back was, purse primly settled on her lap. She watched his secretary knock on the door and go in at the sound of his voice telling her to enter. Not ten seconds later, she came back out. She studied Lisette with more interest as she spoke, telling her that Mr. Linley would see her now.

Lisette thanked her and entered his office, closing the door behind her. The broad, welcoming smile on Byron's face made her heart stutter a bit. He had such an attractive boyish charm about him. His blue eyes always seemed widened with wonder, and his mouth easily curled into an endearing smile. His dark, wavy hair was combed back, perhaps to fit with his new professional image. Lisette missed the way a lock tended to curl into his face.

"Hello, Darling," he greeted with an impish smile. "To what do I owe the immense pleasure? Roberta said you wanted to hire my services. I'm honored."

Lisette pursed her lips and took the seat across from his desk that he gestured toward. Byron leaned back in his chair, observing her with eyes that danced in amusement.

"This is a very serious case, Mr. Linley."

He offered an exaggerated pout. "Mr. Linley? And I thought we were closer than that. I was just about to give you the friends and family discount, Darling."

"Now, see here, I want you to take this seriously!"

He brought his arms up, lacing his fingers behind his head as he narrowed his eyes in scrutiny. "Let me guess, it's about a murder that may have happened on a certain yacht this past weekend? Or was it an accident, as the article I read suggested?"

"I suppose if you could call a gun going off an accident," Lisette said, her voice laced with sarcasm.

A slow smile spread on his face. "Is that what you need me to find out?"

"I need you to find out why there was a gun in the first place."

"There are usually only two reasons to preemptively have a gun, protection or premeditation. I'm not familiar with Troy Turner, but—"

"You already know who the victim was?"

He laughed. "Everyone in Hollywood already knows who the victim was. What kind of private investigator would I be if I didn't know as well? Kudos to Miss Harper for her self-restraint. I'm sure she was devastated not to break the news first."

"Oh, I'm sure she was well compensated somehow," Lisette said bitterly.

"Oh?"

"Never mind that just yet. You were saying something about Troy?"

"Yes. I have to think that since he was invited along on this little sea voyage, Miss Vance didn't consider him too much of a threat. Thus..."

"Premeditation."

"Why are you so concerned with this? Is Olympus thinking of contracting with Verity?"

"No, but I suspect she's thinking of framing me for the murder."

Instantly his hands dropped from behind his head and he sat up straighter. He studied Lisette for a moment, putting that notion together with what he knew about the murder.

"Ahh, I see it now. Clever girl."

"Whose side are you on?"

"Yours always, my darling." He offered a teasing smile, then laced his fingers together in a grip that he settled on top of his desk. "So you want me to find out why Verity Vance shot Troy Turner, I take it? In other words, a motive."

"Yes, that's the gist of it. Herbie assures me that he'll pay any—"

Byron waved her off before she could finish. "This one is on me, Darling."

"Fiddlesticks, naturally you have to be paid for services. And Olympus has plenty of money to—"

"There's only one form of payment I'd like in return."

Lisette glared at him. "If you think I'm going to—"

He began laughing and shaking his head. "I'd forgotten how easy it is to get under your skin, Darling. No, just a dinner date, a *proper* one this time, with real drinks. No more root beers."

"That's no less unsavory, you know," Lisette said, even though she could feel the temperature of her cheeks go up a degree or two with pleasure.

"I never claimed to be a gentleman," he said with a brow arched in villainy.

His grin disarmed her, making her laugh, despite herself. "I can see you aren't planning to be business-like about this at all. I *could* go to prison, you know."

"That won't happen, not under my watch," he said seriously.

"Are you sure you can afford to work for such meager pay?" She allowed her eyes to wander his office. "It seems you now have rent to cover."

"I've made my way in this town. A few cases with very

nice paydays have come my way. Apparently, I'm the go-to man for Hollywood indiscretions of every ilk. I suppose I have you to thank for that. As you implied, studios do have the deep pockets these days. And this case is high profile enough that it should put another tidy little feather in my cap. Now do you feel better about my meager pay?"

She offered a begrudging smile. "I suppose I'm in no position to look a gift horse in the mouth, am I? You're good at what you do and I need all the help I can get."

"So you really think Miss Vance is trying to frame you for this?"

She nodded.

"Okay, then tell me everything that happened this weekend, in detail. Include conversations you had, reactions, moods, everything."

Lisette related the entire weekend as she had for Herbie earlier, giving far more detail. Even when she paused to ask if she was telling him more than he needed to know, he simply shook his head and encouraged her to continue. When she got to the part where Troy was pawing at her face, she was pleased to note a sudden hardness come to Byron's expression. By the end, Byron seemed convinced she had reason to be concerned.

"I think if we can find out the real reason why Verity wanted Troy dead—all the better if it was planned—then all this nonsense about accidents, or worse, framing me, will be harder to swallow. The only obstacle seems to be that, if *Betts* and *Patti* are any indication, then no one will be willing to talk, not if Franklin already got to them. At this point, I think even Leroy might just forget we had an entire conversation on the upper deck while the murder was taking place."

"Not to worry, Lisette, finding secrets is my specialty."

Byron offered a grin. It disappeared as he became serious again. "Now then, who do you suspect is the weakest link, one with the greatest armor against Franklin's meddling, and the least to be swayed by the thirty pieces of silver he may offer?"

"I would say Patricia, but only if she's somehow separated from the pressure of Bethany's influence. Cynthia was the one to actually exclaim that Verity had shot Troy. She didn't seem particularly fond of her even before that. I think if we talk to her, she might be willing to tell us what really happened, even if she may not know the reason why."

"See, you're already thinking like a private detective. It seems we have our first witness to interview."

CHAPTER FOURTEEN

"ARE you sure you don't have other cases to work on?" Lisette asked Byron as they left his office. Roberta had looked askance as he escorted her out of the office, telling her to take messages for any calls that came in.

"Nothing this pressing. A messy divorce that I have a man working on; a photographer paid to camp outside of a certain hotel."

"So that kind of work is beneath you?" She cast a half-cocked grin his way.

"These are desperate times, Lisette. I like to consider myself a man of the people, offer work to those in need. Besides, getting paid to smoke a cigarette and read until you have to take a few shots of some sad sap with his trousers down is nice gigs if you can get it. Trust me, he isn't complaining."

Lisette laughed as he led her to his car. She'd taken a taxi to his office. A frown came to her face as she realized something. "Wait, how are we going to find them? I don't know where the Frosts live."

Byron grinned and turned to face her. "But you know

something about them. Particularly for this time of day. Think, it'll come to you."

She realized he, as usual, was helping her be as good a detective as he was. He'd been some kind of an ace up in San Francisco working for the police department, so she trusted his wisdom. She thought about what she had told him, specifically regarding Cynthia or Neville Frost, mentally replaying everything in her head until—

"Ambrose Westlake! That's where her sons are taking summer classes," Lisette said in a far more excited tone than was proper for the circumstances.

"Very good."

Lisette offered only a brief glare for his patronizing tone. "It's still early, so we might catch her after dropping them off."

"Exactly. So, let's go."

Byron must have spent the past several months memorizing where everything in Los Angeles County was since he needed no directions to get to Ambrose Westlake, located in Beverly Hills. Lisette only knew because she had earned money as a part-time nanny during college, and part of the job required her to chauffeur children to and from schools, including one of the most exclusive in Southern California. Thankfully, she had learned to drive when her family had moved across the country from New York City.

There was a lingering throng of cars ejecting children onto the sidewalk or along the circular drive in front. While most children across the country this time of year were building backyard forts and diving into swimming holes, the children of the wealthy were aiming for excellence. Most were driven in by chauffeurs and Lisette suffered a brief bit of worry that the Frost boys would be likewise carted to school. She dismissed the idea. Anyone desperate for production money wouldn't waste money on a chauffeur for his children, not when either he or his wife was likely capable of driving them.

And there she was.

Cynthia Frost had her hand raised to shield her eyes from the sun that had risen high enough to drench the front of the school in light. Lisette saw her chest rise with a final sigh before she turned to get back into her car idling at the curb. Byron and Lisette rushed to catch her before she got in.

"Cynthia!"

She was at the driver's side door and jerked her head up at the sound of her name. She swiveled it around looking for the source. When her eyes landed on Lisette, they widened in surprise, then panic.

"What are you doing here?" Cynthia practically snarled when Lisette and Byron caught up to her. "I have nothing to say to you."

"Then, I can go to the police." It was the only thing Lisette could think of to keep her from quickly getting into her car and driving off.

It worked enough to get Cynthia to pause and study her through narrowed eyes. "And tell them what exactly?"

"Certainly something different than what I suspect you did." Lisette was guessing now, but based on her experience with Patricia and Bethany, she had to assume Franklin and Verity got to Cynthia or, more likely, Neville.

Cynthia gave Lisette a cynical look. "Just what do you suspect I left out or lied about."

"That you saw Verity shoot Troy." Lisette waited for her to say something or even give some indication that she was correct, but Cynthia remained stoic. "That *is* what you exclaimed when I got back to the dining room from the upper deck."

"The upper deck where you were when the shooting took place?"

"Yes." At least she wasn't claiming Lisette was in the room at the time, holding the gun that shot Troy.

"So you didn't see anything. Well...neither did I. I was simply making assumptions when I said what I said. I was... hysterical." There was a slight grimace on her face as she uttered the last word, as though it irked her to attach such an affliction to herself. Perhaps like many women, Cynthia hated having her state of mind boiled down to such an insulting label.

"But it was obviously Verity who shot him. Unless someone put that gun in her hands and positioned her right over Troy's body."

"I wouldn't know."

"Really, now," Lisette said, feeling her exasperation set in. "Why the sudden change of heart? From what I saw this weekend, you didn't exactly seem to be Verity's best friend. I don't think you even wanted to be there."

"I wish we *hadn't* been there," she spat, as though just mentioning it was a disgusting taste in her mouth.

"And now you're protecting Verity."

"Protecting Verity?" Cynthia gave Lisette an incredulous look. It deepened into something bitter. "I'm *protecting* my family."

"From what?" Lisette asked, hearing the pleading in her voice.

It must have triggered something in Cynthia. A look of panic flashed across her face and she quickly opened her car door and got in. Before Lisette and Byron could even step back away from the curb, she sped off, not caring that there might have been children around. They stood there watching until the car disappeared around the corner.

"I smell something fishy in the air, and it ain't the mackerel," Byron said next to her.

"It just proves my theory, either Franklin threatened her or bribed her. I'm thinking a bit of both."

"Was anyone on that boat incorruptible?"

"Is *anyone* incorruptible? Even you or I would crack under a certain amount of pressure, or be tempted by just the right apple. And Franklin is just the kind of serpent who could apply both, given the resources at his disposal."

"So, we focus on motive instead. As a former detective, it's much easier to get people talking gossip than asking them to act as a witness. People's guards go up at the mere hint of anything official. But you ask about skeletons in the closet of someone else and they're more than happy to accommodate."

"I wish I'd known that before talking to Cynthia. Neville obviously needed Franklin's financial backing more than I thought. It's too bad, as he and Verity are apparently old friends. He's likely to know her secrets, and thus, Cynthia would too. Of the two, she would have been the most likely to tell us."

Byron was already shaking his head. "Ever seen a mama grizzly bear? They'd maul Zeus himself before doing anything that might harm their cubs. Her dislike of Verity has nothing on her wanting to protect her boys. As you just saw."

"I guess it's a good thing she was the only mama bear on the yacht."

"So, out of all the people in attendance, who is least...*maternal*, let's say, but also least likely to be overly influenced by Franklin?"

Lisette thought about it. "Bethany is out, and probably Patricia for the time being. I'm sure the former is sticking close by her side to keep her from talking. We can assume Neville will be as closed-lipped as his wife. We can assume the same for Franklin. Hedley has already shown her cards. Geoff got back to the scene of the crime later than I did, so he wouldn't have seen anything. The members of the band? Well, I wouldn't blame them for having a selective memory in this instance. Franklin probably didn't even need to use his influence on them. That leaves Joann and Lennie. The latter has a much longer history with Verity, based on what I overheard."

"Perfect. I've always wanted to meet Lennie Lamar, but now I have an excuse."

"Not so perfect." Lisette thought back to the way he had looked at Verity all evening. "I'm pretty sure the man is a fool in love."

"Enough to cover for murder?"

"I don't know."

"Well, as you said, anyone is corruptible. What do you think Franklin may have used with him?"

"I don't know, but I may have an idea of how to find out."

CHAPTER FIFTEEN

OLYMPUS STUDIOS HAD a dossier on every important figure in Hollywood. This included most major actors and actresses worth knowing, even those they didn't have contracts with. After all, most studios traded actors every once in a while. They were commodities in the business of making movies, as unsavory as it was to think of it that way. It paid to know everything about what one was getting in a trade.

Lennie Lamar was most definitely an actor worth knowing. Aside from any skeletons he might have in the closet, his dossier would contain all the basic information about him, including his address. As Herbie Hinkle's second in command, Lisette had access to all this information.

"While we're driving, talk to me about your theories on the case. I've found it helps to have a listening ear."

"If you'd have told me Verity would be committing murder this past weekend, I wouldn't have believed you...at first. After only a day and night of being around her, I'm not so sure anymore. She seems rather...manipulative. She has a sneaky way of maneuvering things to go the way she prefers. She also doesn't like any attention being drawn away from her. Still, none of those things spell murder. Half the people in this city are like that."

They arrived at Olympus Studios and were waved onto the lot by the guard, who recognized Lisette. The files were located at a central location maintained by a head librarian of sorts, Lucy Danbury. She managed two employees who did the job of scouring the newspapers and wires to learn any updated information about the people they had on file. She was also responsible for maintaining the master copies of all films made by Olympus Studios. That alone made her one of the most important employees on the lot.

"Good morning, Lucy," Lisette greeted. "I need the files for Lennie Lamar and Troy Turner, the director."

"Would that have something to do with what happened this weekend?" She gave Lisette a piercing look as though hoping she would elaborate as to what happened.

Lisette wouldn't have been surprised if Lucy knew before anyone who had been murdered.

"Unfortunately, I'm not allowed to discuss it." Lucy cast a quick glance to Byron, as though she knew Lisette had been perfectly forthcoming with at least one other person. Lisette thought of something else. "Do you have a file for Verity Vance as well?"

A knowing smile came to Lucy's face. "Sadly, no. For actors and actresses, we only include a file if they've had at least one co-starring role or higher. Obviously, we've decided to begin a file for her, as she's become noteworthy in other ways." Lucy arched a brow but didn't need to elaborate. Right now everyone in the city was probably clamoring to learn more about Verity Vance. Joann may have had a point about her possibly becoming the biggest star Hollywood had ever seen.

"I see," Lisette said, disappointed.

"It's a space issue, you see. I've been trying to get Mr. Huxley to allow us to transfer the files to microform. The *New York Times* has started archiving their papers on something called microfilm developed by Kodak. We try to preserve the paper clippings and photos as best we can, but with continued handling, it eventually deteriorates. We, of course, save a copy of everything we have, in case of fire, but even that doesn't prevent the danger of time. Heaven forbid there's a flood. Microfilm is so much more durable and long-lasting."

"Microfilm. Is that like movie film? That would be pretty flammable no? Studios are constantly in danger of losing copies to fires. At least a few films are gone forever."

"Yes, no storage system is failsafe. That's the main reason we keep our reels off site in a fire-safe structure. You no doubt remember that horrible fire that destroyed nearly all of Empire Studio's reels a little over a year ago," Lucy lamented. "All the more reason to keep files in various formats. Microfilm doesn't have the same flammability problem as movie film. It would also save quite a bit of space, as I suggested. I could hold all the information for several individuals on a single spool the size of a jewelry box. Just think of how much more we could archive. We're getting awfully crowded here now that Hollywood is such a growing industry. Perhaps that could be an incentive Herbie might pass on to Mr. Huxley?"

Lisette grinned, reading the subtext perfectly well. Any cost-saving measure—and cutting down space for storage was an obvious one—was a bonus as far as Mortimer Huxley was concerned.

"I'll see what I can do, Lucy. Thanks."

With a quick nod and a smile, Lucy disappeared into the back room to retrieve the files on Lennie and Troy.

"Here you are, Lisette," she said in a brisk tone, less than half a minute later. The "files" were in two long, flat storage boxes. Lucy was known to keep an exceptional filing system. "We've included the most recent newspaper clippings."

Lisette and Byron took the files to the attached reading room. It was a simple but nicely furnished room with large tables to lay all the files out on and comfortable chairs meant for long sitting sessions. Before casting for any film, an unlucky assistant was tasked with reviewing each file and gathering any relevant information about potential stars, directors, or other important names attached to the project.

"I'll take Lennie. You search Troy," Byron said, sliding Troy's box across the table to her. "See if there's something that sparks a memory with what may have happened this past weekend."

Lisette took it and removed the lid. Lucy had done a fine job of organizing it. On the top was a single sheet that had Troy's basic biographical and contact information. Like many people in Hollywood, his address was in Beverly Hills. There were several articles that hinted at his problems with drinking. He'd gotten into a few fights, went on tirades against actors and producers, and had at least one minor car accident. He'd probably been told by enough people in power to quit, or else. That rule had obviously been ignored over the weekend.

The only other interesting thing that Lisette could find was that Troy had once worked for Titan Studios. It was odd that he and Geoff hadn't at least acknowledged each other more familiarly. Perhaps the head of a studio was too far removed from a director who hadn't done much, or in fact any, work for him in the past five years. Lisette made a mental note to talk to Geoff Dreyfus, should it come to that. Yes, he was the head of Olympus's rival studio, but even that rivalry shouldn't have him relishing the idea of an innocent woman getting the blame for the murder.

"Anything?" Lisette pulled her gaze away from the files she was returning to the box. Byron was leaning back in his chair, intently focused on the papers in his hand as though absorbed in a good book.

It took another verbal prodding before he tore his eyes away to meet hers. He grinned. "Just learning what I can while I have so much information about Hollywood royalty at my disposal. I should work with you more often Lisette, half the work is done for me here, should I ever need to investigate Mr. Lamar, of course."

"Perhaps you'll take that in lieu of our originally agreed-upon payment?"

"Not a chance, Darling." He gave her a wink and quickly pulled himself up, placing all the files back in the box. "As for any ammunition, our Mr. Lamar should be the poster boy for the Boy Scouts. I couldn't find even a speck of dirt."

"Odd for this town."

"So I'm learning. At any rate, I did find one key piece of information, his address."

"So the trip wasn't entirely wasted, it seems."

"Welcome to the world of private detecting. Sometimes the littlest things are found after great effort, and sometimes those little things are the key to it all. Now, let's discover what our comedic fellow has to say about this dastardly deed over the weekend, shall we?"

CHAPTER SIXTEEN

Lennie Lamar lived in a surprisingly modest home in Beverly Hills, at least by the standards of that exclusive enclave. Part of the allure was that it had yet to be annexed into Los Angeles proper. The other part was living in a city where famous names such as Douglas Fairbanks, Mary Pickford, Will Rogers, and, once upon a time, Rudolph Valentino lived.

Lennie's home was a single-story Spanish style that looked almost like a cottage. Yes, it was certainly large by the standards of the average American, but in a town that liked to flaunt its wealth, it seemed rather quaint and cozy. Then again, Lennie wasn't married and had no children, so it was fitting.

Byron drove up the short driveway to the front of the home. There was a pretty garden with flowers still clinging to life that late in the summer. In the height of spring, it was probably stunning.

Lennie met them at the door, leaning against the frame with a sad smile on his face that already hinted he had nothing to offer Lisette.

"I suppose I shouldn't be surprised. In fact, I've been expecting you."

He didn't invite them inside, remaining where he was, his tall frame filling the doorway. Byron leaned against the hood of his car. Lisette stood partially in front of him staring up at Lennie.

"You want to know what I saw Saturday night? I'm afraid I can't help you, Miss Darling."

"Did you spontaneously go blind during the twenty minutes I was gone?"

"I do wish I had seen what led to...well, whatever happened. Perhaps I could have intervened, and Troy would still be alive."

"So there was an altercation?" Lisette offered.

His smile hitched up on one side and he shrugged without comment.

"Could it have possibly been anyone else who shot him? Someone you also didn't have your eyes on?"

"Well, I didn't see *you*."

Lisette pursed her lips, narrowing her gaze at him.

"Don't worry, I have no intention of pointing the finger at you for this, Miss Darling. I know you were outside."

"Is there a threat that the finger might be pointed at me?" It was a mostly rhetorical question, but she wanted to know if that little idea had been dangled by Franklin on top of people forgetting they saw Verity shoot Troy.

"I think...you should stop investigating this." For the first time, he showed an expression of concern. "The answers you're looking for are going to cause a lot of trouble for a lot of people, innocent people, yourself included."

That was an interesting development. What exactly was Lennie holding back?

"And Troy's family? Aren't they innocent in all of this?"

"Troy's family..." He breathed out a quick laugh. "I wouldn't know anything about them. Like me, he's left them far behind."

He grimaced as though that was a sore topic, and quickly changed course. "As I said, I don't know what happened."

"I saw you two arguing, you and Verity. What were you arguing about?"

Lennie simply stared back without an answer.

Lisette tried another avenue of approach. "You and Verity are friends, correct? You've known her a long time. Can you tell me—"

"I think that's all I have to say, Miss Darling." He turned to walk back inside, taking hold of the door to close on them.

"Are you in love with Verity?" Lisette blurted out, thinking quickly.

That got him to stop. He slowly turned to observe her for a long moment. His eyes remained on her for so long, she began to worry something was growing on her face.

"You do look so much like her. Funny how that works out."

"I don't find it particularly funny."

"No, I don't suppose you do," he said with a sigh. He looked off somewhere past her. "I've known Verity longer than most. Almost from the moment she first took a stab at Hollywood. I may have even had a hand in helping her rise through the ranks. I told her it would lead to no good. That she should be happy settling down somewhere else, anywhere else, with a man well-off enough to give her some semblance of the life she wanted. She's beautiful enough for that. But that wasn't Verity. She's too stubborn, too intent on proving something."

"Why wouldn't you want her to be a star? Isn't that the dream of many young women, especially in this town?"

"And many of them find that all that glitters isn't gold." He seemed to find that amusing, a sardonic kind of mirth dancing in his eyes at a secret joke. "My only regret is that she met me during one of her earliest films. She stood out even then. I inadvertently influenced her."

Lisette thought about that, particularly in relation to what he'd said about all that glitters isn't gold.

"Are you talking about her name?"

"Yes," he said cautiously, as though wondering what she might do with that information. "She wanted to change it— thought she would have a better chance with a more memorable name, especially in comedy, which seemed to be her forte. I jokingly suggested she follow my lead. I guess the idea stuck."

Lisette rolled her eyes. "Anyone could have guessed Verity Vance wasn't her real name. It's far too alliterative, like yours. By the time she would have been old enough to work in Hollywood, she would have known your real name wasn't Lennie Lamar. Almost everyone does."

An exposé had been published almost five years ago revealing Lennie's roots in Florida. It also exposed his real name as Leonard Leibovitz. With a name like that, even someone who had never met a Jewish person would have figured out he was, or at least had been raised as such.

Lennie looked out at his garden, then the facade of his home with a proud smile on his face. "Not before I moved here, though."

Lisette wasn't sure what he'd meant about moving. Was he referring to moving to California, or that particular house? Perhaps the original owner or builder had been reluctant to sell to a Jewish person. Some people and places held those kinds of prejudices. The Hollywood industry wasn't one of them, if it ever had been. The Marx brothers were loved by the entire country, if not the world, and they were hardly the only Jewish comedic actors. Even Geoff at Titan was unapologetically Jewish. In this town, it certainly didn't have the same stigma that it did in other parts of the country. Even back in New York, where Lisette had been born and raised, the elite class had placed even the wealthiest Jewish families on a certain echelon, settled well below the Astors and Vanderbilts of the city.

"That's hardly a scandal, Lennie. You and Verity aren't the only actor or actress to change his or her name. Sometimes it even happens without their consent. Just look at John Wayne. Rumor has it he wasn't even present when someone at Fox changed his name from Marion Morrison."

"All the same," Lennie said, focusing his attention back on Lisette as though realizing he may have said too much. "I'm not in love with Verity as you suggested. I just want to protect her. She deserves that much after how hard she's worked to get where she is."

Lisette didn't think being Franklin Winthorpe's girlfriend of the moment took that much work. Perhaps a lot of swallowing one's pride, yes. Still, she didn't say anything out loud, knowing it would fall on deaf if not resentful ears.

"A man has been murdered, Lennie."

"Yes," he coughed out softly, looking none too grief-stricken. "Troy Turner was a fine director. That's about all I can say about the man. Good day."

With that, he did close the door on them. Lisette stared at it, agape for a moment, before turning to Byron.

"What do you think?"

"I think that was a fine interrogation, Miss Darling."

"Not about that, about what he said."

"Well, there's definitely a secret there and it's much more than her name change. He knows what it is." He pushed himself away from the car and walked around to the driver's side.

"We should try to find out for ourselves. It may be her motive. Troy was drunkenly blathering about a secret when I was with him." Lisette got in on the passenger side. "Do you think her name change has something to do with it?"

"Yes, we should definitely learn as much as we can about Miss Vance, but her real name isn't the big secret. Lennie wouldn't have let that slip if it was the thing she's hiding. No, I think we need to focus on what it was Troy knew and how."

Lisette thought about his drunkenly slurred words just before he got handsy: *I know what you are, you little minx. That mask doesn't fool me.*

What had he meant by that? After talking with Lennie, there was perhaps added context, though Lisette still couldn't fathom what it meant.

"You know...it's interesting that Troy said 'I know what you are.' Why not 'who' you are?"

"Or 'where you are' or 'when you are?'"

Lisette slapped him on the arm, even though she laughed. "I'm serious. Do you think it has to do with a prior career? Perhaps at one time, she was more than a girlfriend to men? Maybe she was a felon at some point? I could see her being worried about that."

"Enough to kill for it?"

"It could ruin a reputation. It certainly wouldn't appeal to the average movie viewer. Studios like a clean image, especially since The Code went into effect. It could end her career before it began."

"Then perhaps it's a good thing the Bardess of Burlesque is next on our list. I'm actually looking forward to meeting Joann. I hear she's a card."

"Yes, but the question is, will she be willing to show us her cards?"

CHAPTER SEVENTEEN

JOANN'S ADDRESS was no secret. The rumor of her buying the small apartment building she lived in after the neighbors complained about the parties she threw was well known. She paid each of those neighbors to move out, then turned the whole building into her residence. It made things rather convenient, as there was always a place for party attendees to sleep off an all-nighter.

The building still had the trappings of its former status as a multi-residential building, complete with an intercom at the front door to the building. Joann Golden was the only name, written in gold lettering next to the button for the penthouse apartment. Lisette pressed it and waited.

"Who is it?" Joann's scratchy voice demanded. "If it's another reporter, I've got a nice little twenty-two loaded and ready to put one in your keister. I hope you're wearing armor."

"It's Lisette Darling...from this weekend's—"

She was interrupted by cackling. "It's about time, honey. Come on up."

When the door buzzed to release the lock, Lisette gave

Byron a questioning look. He shrugged and pulled the door open for her. She walked in, happy that they weren't meeting any resistance as they had with everyone else so far.

A housemaid already had the door to the penthouse apartment open for them when they reached the top floor. She led them into a room where Joann sat on a large white sofa, then she silently disappeared. Joann's cigarette holder was in one hand, a trail of smoke leading up from the butt at the end. In her lap sat a tiny chihuahua, who gave three loud yaps. Joann bounced him and he went silent.

"So what number am I?" Joann's mouth curled into a grin.

"I beg your pardon?"

"How many people did ya go to first before coming to me?"

"Well, um—"

"Never mind, I know when I'm not numbero uno on the old dance card. Reminds me of my younger days...and my ex-husband. Come on, have a seat already."

While they sat, Joann set the dog down and it quickly scurried around as though chasing some invisible fly. After a detour to the coffee table, it went back and forth between Lisette's and Byron's feet as they sat in matching armchairs.

"Stop that, Gigi. Leave them alone!"

Gigi decided she liked Lisette's shoes the best and settled into a ball at her feet.

"Huh, how's that for loyalty?" Joann said, shaking her head. "Now, then, I suppose you're wondering what I know from this weekend?"

"Well...yes."

"Despite that detective, or was it an agent, warning us

not to talk to anyone?" The questioning smile on Joann's face was perfectly conspiratorial.

"I know you're not supposed to talk to me about what you saw but—"

Joann waved that away, the cigarette smoke creating a serpent above her head. "Pish-posh, honey. I've never been one to follow the rules."

"Well then," Lisette said, feeling pleased. "What did you see? Surely it was Verity who shot Troy, no?"

Joann laughed. It wasn't her usual cackle, but a softer, almost cynical chuckle. "I would have thought someone in your profession would know better how all of this works. Even murder is game for a bit of negotiating."

"I'm sorry?"

"I think Miss Golden is telling you that she already traded a bit of tit for tat. Either that, or she's waiting to see if you have a better deal for her."

"I think I like the way your mouth works, sonny." Joann gave Byron a coy smile. "But if I was trading tit for tat, I'd be getting a hell of a lot more tat." She did a little jiggle with her upper body in the manner of a burlesque dancer.

"Well, then what did you invite me up for?" Lisette was more than just irritated. "To flaunt it?"

Joann sighed and tapped the growing tail of ash out in a tray. "Listen, honey, I feel for you, but I'm an old lady now. I gotta think about my legacy."

"Is Franklin building a statue in your honor?" Lisette didn't bother hiding her sarcastic contempt.

"No, no statues," Joann said in a surprisingly resigned voice.

"But you're getting your memoir," Lisette finally realized.

Joann shot her a wry smile. "Did it ever occur to you that maybe Troy deserved what he got?"

"Murder? No, Joann, it never occurred to me. No one deserves that."

"Live a little longer and maybe you'll encounter someone who does. I'm not saying Troy deserved that per se, but he wasn't exactly Prince Charming, that one. He had a mean, petty edge to him, and he was the most selfish son of a—"

"Still not a cause for murder, *or* allowing someone else to take the blame when murder is committed."

"Is that what you're here for? You're worried you might take the fall?" Joann laughed, loud and hoarse. "Oh honey, that ain't gonna happen. If it does, then maybe I'll change my tune."

"So you did see what happened, you just won't say so until an innocent woman is on the hook for murder."

Joann simply eyed Lisette as she took a drag from her cigarette holder.

"You said Troy was no Prince Charming, care to elaborate?"

Lisette was grateful for Byron shifting the subject. Lisette was too focused on being framed for the murder, which would lead to no answers. This was at least something Joann might be willing to discuss, and one of their goals was to find a motive for why Verity had shot him. She turned back to Joann to find her shooting Byron a sly smile.

"Are you the beau? He's a keeper, honey." She sighed and tapped her cigarette again before speaking. "Like most men in this industry, he could get a little forward with the girls, maybe a bit handsy. That's nothing new. He's also been known to be dismissive of the help—janitors, maids, and even extras on the set. It was when he was in his cups that the real Troy came out. He was pretty uncensored about his views on things, especially after a few cocktails. *In vino veritas*, as they say. I don't know if you know the story about the poor waiter who spilled wine on him. There's some debate about who ran into whom, my money's on Troy being the offender, but he tore that man down so hard, he made the poor bastard cry. Even got him fired from the job. No small thing in this day and age. The things that came out of his mouth have mostly been hushed up, and he's been pretty good about staying off the sauce the past several years, or at least limiting it. Those looks of his and his skill as a director help him get by, but people remember."

"So he was a mean drunk," Lisette said, unimpressed. She'd seen enough of those in her time. It did explain why he refrained from drinking on the yacht, at least until he finally succumbed.

"That he was. And there wasn't a group out there he didn't have a repugnant opinion about, including women. He's learned to behave himself these past few years, but it rears its ugly head every once in a while."

"And yet, Verity still invited him."

"Because at the end of the day, he's still Troy Turner, the best comedy director around. And let's not claim he's the only one with those views, he was just stupid enough to once upon a time be an itinerant drunk who publicly spouted them. Not many people have the privilege of holding a grudge in this town, even those who share a bed with Franklin Winthorpe."

"Or maybe she simply wanted to murder him."

Joann cackled again. "If so, I have to give it to the gal, she sure knows how to do it with pizazz!"

"I'm sure his family will be relieved to hear that."

"Snakes don't have families, Miss Darling. They're born

and then they slither off to make it on their own. If you're looking for a motive, I'd say it was that forked tongue of his that did it."

"Well thank you, Miss Golden, you've been very helpful." Lisette rose to leave, realizing this had been mostly a fool's errand. All she had learned was that Troy Turner was perhaps not as decent a man as he let on publicly.

Joann chuckled. "Don't be too upset. I have a feeling when the truth comes out about why that girl shot him, it'll be a doozy. Maybe you should be getting your own pound of flesh directly from Franklin."

"Perhaps I should. If I'm going to prison in place of Verity Vance, I deserve *something* from it."

"If you want my advice, take off the gloves, Miss Darling. Everyone in this town has secrets, even yours truly. The only difference is, I'm saving mine for a book deal. You'll eventually have to pay two dollars a pop to see the peep show of my skeletons. Others' secrets may not come so cheaply. Start lifting up the rugs to find the dirt."

Lisette returned a humorless smile as she walked out. Once outside the building, she huffed in frustration, stomping her foot.

"Not very ladylike, Miss Darling," Byron teased.

"Perhaps I'm taking Joann's advice and removing the gloves. A little bare-knuckle action might just be in order, and I don't mean that figuratively."

"Well, before you sully those lovely hands of yours, let's try reading between the lines. After all, she did offer some bit of good advice."

"What was that?"

"We should go to the top, the penthouse level, where a man could afford to hold a grudge."

"Geoff Dreyfus? He didn't see anything."

"But he has worked with Troy Turner, at least until he stopped working with him. I think we should find out why."

Lisette felt her hope reignite, then falter. "He's the head of Titan Studios, Olympus's main rival. I doubt he'll talk to me just to reveal why his company stopped working with Troy."

"I think, under the circumstances, he might just make an exception."

CHAPTER EIGHTEEN

GEOFF DREYFUS DID INDEED MAKE an exception to see Lisette and Byron. In fact, Lisette was surprised at how quickly and easily he acquiesced to a meeting in his office when she called.

Geoff was seated at his desk and met Lisette and Byron with an assessing look as soon as his secretary led them in. She wasn't surprised by the outlandish size of his office, taking up nearly the entire top floor of the most imposing building on the Titan Studios lot. She was impressed by how tastefully modern it was decorated, mostly white and gold Art Deco with interesting pieces of art and antiquities on display. Geoff was obviously a fan of Ancient Egypt.

As Lisette and Byron took the two seats across from him at his desk, Geoff leaned back in his chair, eyes narrowing even more. "I suppose I don't have to ask why you wanted to meet me."

"You didn't really give me a chance to say when I called."

"I assumed it was about what happened to Troy Turner. In which case, I'm just as curious as you are. Which begs the question of why you've come to me. As you know, I wasn't in the room when he was shot."

"Are you sorry he's dead?" Lisette studied him as hard as he was studying her, waiting to see if he would give away any tells regarding his true feelings about the man.

"Am I a suspect now as well?" Geoff said, a heavy dose of humor in his voice.

Lisette eyed Byron, who returned a blithe smile and gestured as if to give her the floor to ask the questions. She turned back to Geoff.

"Why did Troy stop directing pictures for you?"

Geoff's brow rose in surprise. "My, my, you have done your research. Perhaps I should stop trying to lure Herbie away from Olympus and go after you."

Lisette couldn't help a small smile. It was always a pleasure to be flattered in the way that mattered to her. The smile disappeared when she remembered the gravity of the circumstances.

"It's no secret," Geoff said easily. He sat forward again to rest his intertwined hands on the desk. "I had no interest in working with someone who held such bigoted views."

"What?" Lisette was surprised at how frank he was about it. Joann had confessed Troy held certain views, but it seemed Geoff wouldn't be so coy about revealing them.

"Oh, he's been a good boy for some time now. Keeping his nose clean and his mouth shut, but I know the truth."

"What is it you heard or saw?"

"Beverly Hills."

Lisette's brow wrinkled in confusion. What kind of answer was that?

"Created almost thirty years ago, a perfectly planned community of perfectly planned homes...and perfectly planned people. Of a certain ilk, of course."

Now, Lisette was catching on. Perhaps this was what Lennie had been talking about. Hopefully, Geoff would explain further.

"Restrictive covenants preventing members of the, ah, kosher subset of the population from owning or buying homes in the city. We aren't the only restricted group, of course. And who was one of the most vocal proponents of keeping it that way? None other than a particular resident of that very fine city—or should I say, *former* resident?"

"So Troy wanted to keep Jews from buying homes in Beverly Hills?"

"He's on the record, or at least he was five years ago. A dumb move in this town, but some people's heads are too big for their shoulders. Other studios—Olympus included—may offer him a slice of the pie. This includes men of my own ilk, who I suppose are happy to ignore that slight. The bakery here at Titan was officially closed for business as far as Troy Turner was concerned."

"Well, I suppose that's a good enough reason not to work with him." Lisette wondered if it was a good enough reason for murder. "Was Verity Vance secretly Jewish?"

Geoff erupted with laughter. "Now, that would be a surprise. That girl is about as Jewish as a pork chop dinner. Not many members of the tribe hail from Louisiana."

"She's from Louisiana?"

"Or so my sources say."

"Why would you have Verity checked out?" Byron interjected, sitting up with sudden curiosity.

Geoff slid his eyes to him then back to Lisette. "I'm sure you, of all people, know exactly why I was on that yacht this weekend. I suppose that's no secret either. It's a good deal, Titan Studios joining Winthorpe Media. They tap into the film-making market, and we get the kind of positive nationwide publicity most studios would clamor for, all without having to beg for it. Morty missed a rare opportunity, passing that up. Maybe he should go to Rutherford Heart up in his palace by the sea." Geoff laughed once again.

"But you did your due diligence," Lisette confirmed. "Anyone tied so closely to Franklin was worth investigating."

"Naturally." Geoff spread his hands as though that much was obvious. "Franklin is, well, not an ideal partner to work with. Thank goodness Edgar is the true head of that media empire. Yes, there's a bit of unfortunate history with the Winthorpe name, but nothing that will sully the Titan name, even by association. All the same, I don't like surprises. Franklin seemed to be silly for that dame." He shook his head in wonder. "I, however, am not a fool. I wanted to know more about Miss Vance before I even stepped foot on that boat."

"What did you discover?" Lisette sat up, realizing she might learn something useful.

"Not much. Whatever she did to clean up her past, she did it well. Miss Marie LeBlanc is squeaky clean."

"So, that's her real name?"

"According to the State of California, where she's registered as a resident. Mind you, I didn't do an entire in-depth biography of the woman. She could still have all sorts of dirt floating down the Mississippi River that I don't know about. She was a secondary concern. Thankfully, Franklin seems to have cut his ties to her. Never let a woman drag you down with her."

"He has? He told you that?"

"I asked him directly. If he was going to be sitting in a courtroom defending an obvious murderer, I'd have serious misgivings about hitching the Titan wagon to his horse. He assured me that he wanted nothing more to do with the woman. Seemed rather bitter about it all, from the look of things."

"I'd imagine finding out the gal you'd been seeing is a murderer might do that."

"You'd think. But the change of heart was only just this morning. Yesterday, he was singing a different tune."

"And he didn't say what had changed his mind?"

"No, only that he'd make sure the Winthorpe reputation, and thus Titan, wouldn't be sullied."

"How early this morning did you two talk?" Byron asked.

"Early. I start my day at six in the morning and made sure a message was left with him to call me first thing. I don't think the man slept, because that's exactly when the call came in."

Lisette pondered that. Everyone she had talked to had been well after that time. Perhaps Franklin hadn't had a chance to renege on all of his promises or threats.

"And you have no idea what may have made him bitter? I mean, if it wasn't the murder itself."

"It wasn't that. I asked, he refused to answer."

"Perhaps he was embarrassed about it and didn't want to say?" Lisette offered, wondering if Geoff was simply being deliberately vague.

"More than being the sugar daddy of a killer?" He seemed incredulous.

"You'd be surprised."

Geoff laughed. "I doubt that. I've seen enough scandals in Hollywood to fill a book. Frankly, these days people could stand to be a bit more embarrassed about things."

"Perhaps it's a good thing he finally is," Lisette said mostly to herself.

"Listen," Geoff said, drawing her attention back to him. "I have an idea why you might be worried. I don't think it was an accident, Verity inviting you onto that yacht. You two could practically be sisters, if not twins. I think the girl is dangerously cunning, and you sadly fell right into the trap she set. Those masks? That was just the extra insurance. It's good you have Herbie in your corner. He'll do right by you."

"I'd have felt better about things if you'd been in the room."

"Odd that I wasn't," he said with a sardonic smile.

"Is there anything else you can think of that may help discover why Verity shot Troy?"

"Offhand, no. But, despite who you work for, if I do think of or learn anything, I'll give you a call."

"Thank you," Lisette said with a smile of appreciation.

She and Byron rose to leave.

"So what did you think of that?" Lisette asked once they were outside. "You certainly are leaving it to me to do all the questioning."

"Because you do it so well. You asked everything I would have asked if I was getting paid. You're much closer to the situation than I am, so it's fitting. In fact, I think everything we learned today is best discussed over a nice, juicy steak and a bottle of wine."

"I'm hardly in the mood for courtship, Byron."

"Consider it a work dinner," he said, taking her arm in his as he led her back to the car. "There will be plenty of time for courting when this is all over. For now, I'm going to do a little sleuthing to earn my dinner with you. You go back to Herbie and help him handle those fires at Olympus."

"How can I work when all of this is going on?"

"You'll simply trust that I'm doing what I need to, and rest easy. I'll pick you up at eight tonight. Dress...swanky."

"You're thinking about juicy steaks and nice dresses all while I may be facing a lifetime in prison...or worse."

"If it's your last meal, I'm happy it's with me, Darling. But don't worry, doll, I shall do my best to keep that from being the case."

CHAPTER NINETEEN

When she returned to Olympus Studios, Lisette told Herbie about all her morning interviews with Byron at her side.

"Sadly, it does seem as if Franklin has been meddling. Interesting about this change of heart Geoff mentioned— good of him to speak with you, by the way. I wonder what the dear fellow may have learned about our murderess to view her through a less rosy lens."

"I'm sure it has to do with why she murdered Troy. I doubt Franklin will tell me though."

"Well, you have a good partner in Byron. If he says he's working on it, trust him."

"You certainly have a high opinion of him." Lisette offered a wry smile.

"I know quality when I see it. I hired you, didn't I?"

That was enough to make her laugh and lift her mood just a bit. The rest of the day, Herbie had enough work to keep Lisette occupied. She did wonder if he had deliberately piled her plate to keep her from thinking too much about the murder.

Lisette got home later than usual and was instantly accosted by Darcy.

"How was it today? Did you learn anything more? The evening papers have finally announced it was Troy Turner who was murdered."

"Of course they have. That secret wasn't going to be kept for too long. I spent all morning trying to figure out why he was killed."

"Obviously it's because they were former lovers. That's the number one reason women kill. Well, there's self-defense of course. But premeditated murder? Yep, definitely a broken heart or jealousy."

"I do believe Euripides wrote a play about that. I suppose it's a good thing Troy had no children with Verity."

"Who is Euripides?"

"He's Greek."

"Well, I don't know about the Greeks, but last year I read a story in...well, I forget which magazine it was. But anyway, a wife killed her husband and set it up so his *mistress* took the fall! She almost got away with it, except the mistress had been cheating on the husband with someone else at the time! How about *that*?"

"One might almost be inclined to think of sin as a virtue." Lisette sighed and fell back on the sofa. Isabelle took that as a sign to commandeer her lap and demand a bit of petting. Lisette happily complied, enjoying the way it soothed her mind.

"So, what did everyone have to say? Surely someone saw Verity shoot him?"

"No one who was willing to admit to it."

"*Really?*" Darcy was aghast.

"Really. I'm having dinner with Byron tonight to discuss it."

"*Finally,* you two are going on a proper date. I swear Lisette, the way you dangle men around."

"It's not a date, and I don't dangle men. I have a career and goals to think of."

"Good grief, if I had your looks, I'd be just like Verity and get myself a millionaire, easy. Some gals have all the luck."

"First of all, you're adorable, Darcy. Any man would be lucky to have you. Second, Verity obviously wasn't all that lucky if she had a reason to kill. I just have to find out what that reason is."

"I don't get it. With looks like that, who could have touched her? Even Franklin got everyone to shut up about being a witness. Whatever secret she has it must have been a doozy. What do you think it is?"

"I have no conceivable idea...yet."

"*Ohh,* maybe her father was a spy in the war! Or maybe her mother ran a bordello. Maybe she poisoned the town's water supply back home?"

"Or perhaps she's from another planet or the lost city of Atlantis," Lisette said with a laugh. "Either way, I should take a bath and change for my *non-date.*"

Lisette rose from the couch, eliciting a mewl of reproach from Isabelle who leaped to the floor. As she bathed, Lisette thought about Darcy's absurd suggestions. She had been correct in stating that pretty women got away with a lot more than they should have. Even the murder of a popular director could have been excused, given the proper context, no matter how contrived it was. Perhaps that would be Verity's defense?

At eight o'clock on the dot, Byron arrived. Lisette was dressed swanky as requested, and quickly ran out to meet him. She didn't want him coming up to face Darcy's suggestive remarks about this being a romantic date. How could it be when it was obtained in such a mercenary manner? And the topic of the evening hardly encouraged any amorous ideas.

Byron drove her to a very nice steakhouse, the kind with proper red leather booths, dark wood, and candlelit lighting.

"Please tell me you've miraculously discovered Verity's motive," Lisette said after he ordered a bottle of wine for them once they were seated.

"My day was fine, thank you for asking, Lisette. How was the rest of your day?"

"You know how it was. I was on pins and needles thinking the police were one moment away from putting the cuffs on me," Lisette replied testily. She was no less irked by the way he laughed in response. "I'm glad you find that funny."

"I don't. I also don't think you're one step away from being arrested. Not yet, at least."

"I feel so reassured. What did you learn?"

"There are only three Marie LeBlancs registered in the State of California, one of which is most likely our gal."

"Well, we knew that much."

"What we didn't know is that one of them is a LeBlanc by marriage, the second was born here...seven years ago, and the third arrived here four years ago...at the age of fifteen."

"Fifteen? So, Verity is only nineteen years old?" Lisette was surprised. "That's odd. Usually, actresses claim to be younger than they really are. The only reason to claim to be older is to get work before you're of age."

"Also, at fifteen she would have been unable to rent an apartment or buy a home. I decided to dig up where she was staying back then, and with whom. It was an apartment leased under the name of Neville Frost."

"Neville? If his children are now old enough to go to Ambrose, he would have definitely been married to Cynthia four years ago. He doesn't seem the type to have a kept woman, certainly not someone like Verity. She seems more...ambitious than that."

"Perhaps she was desperate? Taking advantage of a weak-willed man?"

"Or perhaps it was something other than a bit of hanky-panky? She comes from Louisiana. He has an accent, which I'll bet he got in Louisiana. Maybe they both knew each other back home. It would at least explain why she claimed he was one of her oldest friends. But even in a friendship, it's asking a bit much to provide a home."

"Maybe they're related?" Byron offered.

"He's in his mid-thirties, so it's *possible* she could be a daughter—some teenage romance. Or, she could be a half-sibling; the result of an affair or a second marriage?"

"That would make him awfully generous. From what I've seen, that's usually cause for resentment rather than affection between the children."

Lisette was much closer to her father than her mother, but she would have probably resented him having an affair or leaving to start a new family. She had to imagine that anyone who was the result of an affair or even a second marriage might not be ecstatic about it either. But some people were simply more forgiving than others.

"So we should investigate any Frosts in Louisiana? That shouldn't be too hard. It's a tad Anglo-Saxon for a former French territory."

"Perhaps Verity wasn't the only one to change her

name. If the secret hails from back home, and Neville is tied to it, he may have wanted to change his name as well."

"Cynthia did seem to be bitter about attending the party. She's certainly not Verity's biggest fan. Also, that business about protecting her family. She may not want anyone digging too deeply into the Frost or Leblanc family tree. I can understand wanting to escape your past."

Byron stared back with a hint of sympathy in his eyes. "At least you didn't have to change your name."

"True." Lisette wallowed in a short trip down memory lane before shaking that bad business away. It was another life back in New York, losing a relative to murder. She usually tried not to dwell on it too much. "But we don't know that Neville changed his name, or that he's even related to Verity."

"That's what detective work is. Driving down roads only to meet a dead end. Thank goodness the brain doesn't charge for gas."

"So we investigate Neville Frost's family, presumably from Louisiana. *Then*, we dig deeper into Verity's past. *Then,* hope we find a motive? Isn't the bigger question how Troy even knew about any of this, and that's *if* it's even related to why she shot him?"

"What does your instinct say?"

"My instinct?"

"Yes, I've found women have much better intuition than men. Tell me the first thing that comes to your mind when you think of a reason why Verity would shoot Troy. Especially with everything you've learned about her and him and all that's tied to the murder."

"It's this secret of hers, a secret she would kill for." She thought back to him pulling her mask up from her face. "He looked at me in surprise, as though I wasn't what he was expecting. I just assumed it was because he originally thought I was Verity. What if it was something else that surprised him?"

"Such as?"

"Something that can be hidden by a mask?" Lisette shook her head in thought, remembering. "People like to hide who they truly are...or just reflect the real person deep inside...."

"What are you pondering?" Byron asked with an expectant smile.

Lisette considered him. "How do you feel about jazz?"

CHAPTER TWENTY

LISETTE AND BYRON finished their steak dinner, moving on to more pleasant fare once they realized they were talking in circles about the murder, all with no answers to be had. At least, not yet.

They may have hurried a bit at the end, skipping dessert in their eagerness to head to the Satin Club. It was Monday night, when many places decided to stay closed. But money was money, and people rarely took a break from drinking or entertainment. All the same, there wasn't a line to get in on the first workday of the week. Lisette figured that would change come Friday night.

She had never been inside the club. It wasn't much to look at, especially with fewer people to hide the black walls, which could have used a fresh coat of paint, and floor that was scuffed from too much dancing. It was rather seedy, but then again, that was probably part of the appeal—particularly for pampered princesses who wanted to try something a bit more daring. Even on a slow night, they weren't the only white customers, though there certainly weren't any young socialites slumming it that evening.

They were led to a table near the front, where a man sat at a piano playing some mellow tune rather than jazz. Perhaps that was more fitting for a Monday evening.

Lisette stopped the hostess before she could return to her post at the front door. "I'm looking for a man who usually plays the trumpet here, Leroy?" She realized she had never gotten his last name.

There was a slight glimmer of a knowing look as she mentally categorized Lisette. It faltered as the woman's eyes darted to Byron next to her. They became more uncertain, more cautious.

"He ain't playing tonight, ma'am."

"Oh, that's too bad. I suppose I'll have to come back tomorrow. I needed to speak with him about something important."

The woman studied her for a moment, as though wondering whether to give her more information. Lisette decided to give her some encouragement.

"It's nothing bad. I'm certainly not trying to get him into trouble. We were just having a conversation at one point about a club back in New York we both knew, the Peacock Club? He told me I should stop by here if I ever wanted to learn more about clubs in Los Angeles."

She tilted her head and exhaled softly, as though already regretting what she was about to say. "He usually comes in Monday to collect his pay. You might catch him if you stick around a while."

"Really?" She made sure to visibly brighten. "Thank you."

The woman gave a quick nod and rushed back to her post, eager to escape more questions.

"I suppose that means listening to music and drinking while we wait for payday," Byron said before catching the eye of a waitress to order drinks. "There are certainly worse ways to do my job."

After ordering they continued to talk more about their families.

"My father had Harlan and me up early each morning to help out in the orange grove. It was certainly a stark change from New York, especially having grown up with money, but I loved it. Back in Queens, we had no yard, not even a tree. There's something to be said for the city, but nothing beats fresh air. And the long drive there, across America, was life-changing. They've sold the orange grove and now just live on a small ranch near Fresno."

"From New York City to the middle of California. That really must have been something. I've spent most of my life in or near San Francisco. I was too young to remember the fire that destroyed the city back in '06 but I lost an uncle I never got a chance to know. My father would go around the city, pointing out what used to be where with a forlorn look in his eyes. That's about the only tragic story in my life."

"It must be something to see the city that you once knew, completely gone. I can't imagine New York being burned to the ground; having to rebuild from scratch. So much history, gone."

"History is about rebuilding. Progress, they call it. How many old mansions have now been replaced by apartment buildings out there?"

"I haven't been back since...well, since we left. I'm sure it looks completely different now."

Before Lisette could say more, her eyes caught a familiar face entering the club. Leroy chatted up the hostess, who flashed a smile that hinted she would have enjoyed something more than idle conversation. It faded when she gestured into the club, pointing right at the table Lisette and

Byron were sharing. Leroy's eyes slid their way and narrowed with dismay. Lisette, undaunted, smiled and waved him over. He seemed to think twice about it before sighing and ambling their way.

"Miss Darling." His voice was neutral, as was his demeanor, giving nothing away.

"Why don't you join us for a drink?"

"The help doesn't mix with the clientele."

She wasn't sure if that was a firm rule or just an excuse. "Is there somewhere we can talk?"

"I don't think that's a good idea. Besides, I'm not sure we have anything to discuss." His gaze was rich with meaning. It wasn't just that he hadn't seen anything, it was that he knew better than to say anything even if he had. That didn't bode well for her getting anything from the rest of the band, who had actually been in the room at the time of the shooting.

"It's not about what happened this weekend."

Puzzlement flickered in his dark eyes. "Then, what did you want to discuss?"

"Pampered princesses?"

He exhaled with mild exasperation. "This won't lead to no good, you know."

Lisette could see he was on the cusp of agreeing, so she said nothing. He slid his eyes to Byron, and for some reason, he seemed to relax, then nodded. "Let's go on out back. This is no conversation for inside ears."

Lisette quickly stood to follow him, Byron doing the same. Now, she understood why Leroy felt better about Byron being there, especially if they were going to a back alley.

In the back of the club, they had their privacy. Leroy leaned against the wall and pulled out his pack of cigarettes.

He tapped one out and lit it, taking a long draw before releasing the smoke. "Ask away, then."

"Did Verity hire you for the yacht party?"

He shook his head. "Her friend, the blonde, Patti. She comes here often enough. She was the one who offered us the gig."

"So you'd never met or seen Verity before then?"

"She came in once, maybe twice. I s'spect this wasn't her kinda place." A sardonic smile spread his mouth around the cigarette. "She didn't take a shine to the lighting, I suppose."

"Is that code for something?"

"Isn't everything?"

"Care to crack the code for us?" Byron said with a wry smile.

Leroy considered them for a moment. "Listen, I don't know why your girl shot that man, and frankly, I don't like making it any of my business. My boys already got sore thumbs from the screws the police are putting on them, not to mention those g-men. They need those thumbs to play."

"And they can't just say what they saw?" Lisette hinted.

"No, ma'am, they can't." He gave her a level look.

"What do you know about Patti—Patricia?"

"She's good folk. Comes in for a harmless bit of fun, doesn't cause problems. Not until now, anyway. She at least had the courtesy of apologizing."

"She did? When?"

He winced, realizing he'd given something away. "This morning."

"How'd she know where to find you?"

"She knows me well enough to know my day job." He didn't tell them what that was, and Lisette decided it was irrelevant. No need to have them detouring down pointless roads.

"Did she say anything else about this weekend?"

"I can't rightly remember." Lisette didn't need an interpreter for that—she was getting nothing about the murder by picking at this particular thread.

"What *can* you remember? Anything leading up to the shooting?"

Leroy chuckled and shook his cigarette her way. "Now you're askin' the right questions, or at least gettin' there."

"Does that mean you'll answer?"

He took a moment to take another drag from his cigarette. "Listen, I didn't hear or see anything. Anyone comes asking, that's what me and my boys will say...on the record. Off the record, there are a few clues as to what exactly was going on this weekend, at least when combined with everything else."

"What clues?" Lisette asked, a mixture of impatience and hope in her voice.

He considered her for a long moment, then looked off to the side, working his jaw in thought. "It's not my place to say, not like this. Not even in the case of murder. But..." He laughed softly and shook his head. "I have to give it to the girl, she knows how to play a good one on people."

"And yet, I fail to find the humor."

He eyed her. "No, I don't suppose you would, especially seeing as you might just find yourself entangled in all of it."

"So you know she was setting me up?"

"Not at first, no. Maybe she was, or maybe you just became convenient after the fact." He shrugged.

"You think there might be another reason?"

"That one I'm not going near, no ma'am. But people talk, and word gets around. But who really knows the truth?

It's like that game I heard you all played on the boat. What started as one thing becomes something completely different by the time it reaches my ears. Still, there's enough to suss out exactly what's going on, and what happened back home."

"Back home in Louisiana?"

He arched a brow in surprise. "So you know that much, huh?"

"I'd like to know more."

"I'm sure you would."

"And you won't tell me, even if it means Franklin pressuring people into maybe saying I was the one who shot Troy?" It hadn't yet reached that stage but if Leroy was going to be so ambiguous, Lisette didn't mind muddling the truth a bit to get answers.

He twisted his mouth to the side, then sighed. "I suppose I can help you out a bit. You should look into who that gal really is."

"We've *been* doing that. We haven't found much, just that she's younger than she claims to be, only nineteen, she changed her name to Verity Vance from Marie LeBlanc, and she's from Louisiana."

"You did your research into *Marie LeBlanc*, I see." He chuckled at some thought only he was privy to. "I can tell you this, the kind of investigating you folks do wouldn't find what it is she's hiding. You have to go deep into the swamps and bayous of Louisiana, and even then, you won't find people who will say a word against her. Jaws clamped shut tighter than an alligator on a catfish, especially when it comes to anything on the record, and *especially* when it comes to outsiders. That's how things work down there. There's a certain code for people like Miss Vance, or should I say Mademoiselle LeBlanc. Frankly, I fall into that camp as well. My people come from down south too. We don't break that code."

"Well this has been helpful Mr.— Golly, I realize I never got your last name. I suppose it would be breaking code to tell me that?"

His mouth curled into a smile. "Mr. Johnson."

"Mr. Johnson. Thank you so much for your help. I'll be sure to send a thank you card when I'm on trial for murder instead of Verity—oops, I mean Marie."

"That woman ain't going to no trial, not if she knows what's good for her." His accent was getting heavier, as if to stress a point. "But just to ease your mind, I will say this, the answer, it was right there on that big boat the whole time if you paid attention."

"That's quite possibly the most indecipherable thing you've said thus far." Lisette threw up her hands in frustration.

"It was there. Pay close attention to all those folks at that little party, including those masks. You of all people might be able to figure it out. Just find out the real reason she invited you on that boat. If I'm right—and I don't know for sure that I am, you see—it wasn't because she planned on murder. I don't think she expected that at all. That would have been dancing a little too close to the Devil's tail, even for someone as devilish as that dame."

Before Lisette could ask any more questions, Leroy pushed away from the wall. With his cigarette still in his mouth he tipped his hat to Byron and her.

"If you don't mind, I have some money to collect. Salutations and good night to you folks."

Lisette watched him go back into the club, her mouth open in appalled frustration. "I'm pretty sure I have even more questions now than before we got here."

"So do I, but the good news is, at least we have a better map to navigate us down the right road."

"What does that mean?"

"It means, we need to review that party with a fine tooth comb and discover the real reason Verity invited you on that boat. So let's start driving, Miss Darling."

CHAPTER TWENTY-ONE

LISETTE SHOULD HAVE BEEN HOME asleep, as it was still a Monday night and she had a job to do in the morning. Herbie would have, of course, been understanding about it if she took time off to investigate Verity's crime, but she saw no reason why that woman should interfere with her life any more than she already had.

Byron was enough of a gentleman not to suggest either his apartment or hers. Instead, they settled on his office. He poured whiskey for both of them. Though that wasn't her usual choice of drink, Lisette accepted, hoping it would jumble her mind enough that something might accidentally settle into place.

"Okay, so let's look at this party, shall we?"

"He didn't say it was necessarily the party, he just said something on that boat. In fact, he said it was there the whole time if I paid attention."

"Good point," Byron grinned at her. "Look at you being a brilliant detective. So, what was there the whole time?"

"Verity? Me? The guests? The crew? The Pacific Ocean? Those awful cocktails were pretty prevalent.

Honestly, I've replayed that entire party in my head and I can't pinpoint what might give me the answer."

"Leroy seemed to think you should know more than anyone else. What was her interaction with you like?"

"Limited. She greeted me, and pointed out we could almost be twins—in fact, she wasn't the only one to say as much."

"So...perhaps it has something to do with family? Or perhaps the way you look?"

"The secret couldn't possibly be that she's not really a blonde," Lisette said with a sarcastic laugh.

"Perhaps..." Byron stopped, his face indicating he was hesitant to express his thought.

"What? Whatever it is, it couldn't possibly be worse than going to prison for a murder I didn't commit."

"Maybe her history isn't the only one involved in a game of telephone. Maybe she picked you, not because of what you look like or who you are, but because of similar pasts?"

"You think she knows about the murder in my family?" Lisette sat up straighter in shock.

"It wasn't difficult for me to learn. There was a lot of press surrounding it at the time. Maybe she did her own investigation."

"But why?" As soon as she asked the question, she knew the answer. It played right into Verity's possible premeditation for Troy's murder.

"Were you ever a suspect in that murder?"

"Everyone in my family was. In fact, I even..." Lisette swallowed hard, thinking of the prank she and her younger cousins had played at the time. It sometimes made her want to cry, wondering if perhaps it may have inadvertently played a role, despite everyone's assurances at the time. It was still difficult to fathom that one of her own family members had killed the other, and all during some silly seance.

Byron stared at her with sympathetic eyes. "What?"

"I was just thinking about what I used to be like before that night. That fourteen-year-old was playful, mischievous...rebellious. I've become this play-by-the-rules woman now that I'm older."

"Nothing wrong with that. Especially after what you went through. Still, I'll bet there's more of that girl in you than you think. I believe I'm going to have a fine time drawing her out."

Lisette pursed her lips, biting back a smile. After so many years playing strict schoolmarm to troublesome actors and actresses, the idea of being a bit troublesome herself had a certain appeal.

"At any rate, the person who committed that crime is serving their time," she insisted. "There was no word of mouth or game of telephone to blur the truth. Even the papers put it right there in black and white. I'm no murderer."

"Sometimes all it takes is being in the orbit of murder to get people talking. You'd be surprised at the nefarious plants that grow from tiny seeds planted just the right way."

"So you think that's what she's doing? Planting those seeds?"

"I don't know, but it is something to consider. We'll set that aside for now."

"I don't want to, I want to—"

"It was just a thought, Lisette."

"You're trying to spare my feelings now. I'd rather rip every bit of it to shreds to prepare myself."

"Alright, then. As you said, you were never found guilty. If anything, you have a better understanding of the horrors of murder. So, let's not wander down that road at the expense of others."

Lisette settled her nerves and took a breath. "Okay, as you said, it was quite possibly the similarities in the way we look. I don't know why she'd want someone who looks almost exactly like her on board. She doesn't seem like the type who enjoys competition. She even sat me right next to Franklin at dinner."

"Yes, that did seem odd. I'm still trying to figure that one out."

"That makes two of us."

"Perhaps she was sick of being Franklin's gal and hoping to push someone else on him?"

Lisette coughed out a laugh. "Why on earth would she do that, especially before he helped her make it in Hollywood? Any smart woman would milk him for as long as possible. Besides, if she'd done even the slightest investigation into that plan, she would have known I'd be the last woman on Earth, let alone Hollywood, to even entertain that idea."

Byron's brow rose. "Perhaps *that* was the point. You were safe enough to sit next to him."

"So why invite me at all? When I tried to ask her, she quite smoothly shifted the topic and made her escape." Lisette growled in frustration, earning a look of amused surprise from Byron. "Oh stop, I don't care if it's unladylike. I feel like we're right on the cusp of knowing the answer. Like Leroy said it's right in front of us, but we're just missing it, like those hidden picture puzzles."

"In which case, let's pull back. We should return to the opposite side of this coin: Troy Turner. Let's work on why he may have been the target of her gun. We'll start at the beginning. What was he like when he first boarded?"

"He seemed fine. He arrived and greeted Verity with a kiss on each cheek. She seemed pleased, and he was charming as ever. No sign of any tension between them. He remained that way through lunch. Then dinner came along and he seemed more...thoughtful, I suppose. I'd taken a nap all afternoon, so I have no idea what it could have been that changed things."

"None? What was everyone else doing?"

"Watching that collection of all Verity's prior roles on film, small as they were. The nap may have been a convenient excuse to miss that bit of fluffing." Lisette was about to take a small sip from her glass but stopped. "You know, Betts—Bethany mentioned something about Troy ignoring her, or at least not getting distracted by her deliberate flirting. I dismissed it as nothing more than her usual grousing, but what if Troy was distracted by something far more interesting than Verity's acting repertoire?"

"A particular movie he saw her in?"

"Patricia said there were films shown that she'd forgotten Verity had been in. Also, I have to say, Verity did seem less than thrilled with the fact that Franklin had put together all of her work for viewing. Again, I had just dismissed that as Verity being Verity. But what if she wasn't just ungrateful? What if she was truly upset? Franklin had said it was a surprise for her, after all. He probably thought he was doing her a favor, showing her range of acting."

"Maybe it showed less than stellar performances? We men can sometimes be perfectly clueless, you know."

Lisette smiled, but shook her head. "I doubt that. Even a foolish man like Franklin would have known better than to profile any performance he knew Verity would be ashamed of. Still, perhaps there is one he wouldn't have had reason to believe she should be ashamed of. A film that led Troy to discover something about her."

"So we need to get a hold of that reel."

"If Franklin knows it's what led to the murder, he probably dropped it in the ocean. Along with that gun, most likely. He certainly wouldn't agree to a meeting with us to hand it over."

"So how do we find out what was shown during that screening?"

"He had to have hired someone to put it together. That meant going to all the studios to get copies...including Olympus." Lisette felt her excitement grow. It was tempered by the hour of the night. "They would have had to go through Lucy, and she won't be there this time of night."

"I suppose you know where your first stop is in the morning," Byron said, lifting his glass toward her. Lisette lifted hers with a smile, finally realizing there might be a light at the end of this mysteriously dark tunnel.

CHAPTER TWENTY-TWO

THE NEXT MORNING, Lisette was eager to interrogate Lucy, or simply ask her who may have requested copies of films Verity Vance—or Marie LeBlanc—had even been an extra in. Hopefully she had also gotten around to compiling the dossier on Verity, which would have included a list of all such films.

That plan was thwarted by the headline that filled the morning newspapers: **Body of Actress From Deadly Yachting Trip Found in West Hollywood.**

Herbie had all the major papers delivered to their office every morning. All the local papers had some version of that headline somewhere on the front page. "Actress" certainly hooked more eyes than the name of said unknown actress: Bethany Ford.

Lisette eagerly grabbed the first paper on the pile and scanned through the article, reading it a bit more slowly the second time. Her body had been found in a park in West Hollywood and she'd been hit in the head. The authorities were treating it as foul play, though they wouldn't know for sure if it had been an accident or murder until they had a suspect. Still, the timing was awfully convenient.

To everyone except Lisette.

Verity had still been in custody Monday evening, as the article had so helpfully pointed out. It was the perfect alibi.

"I see you've learned the *Veni Vidi Vici* saga continues," Herbie said, arriving at the office not too long after her. He hung his hat and passed through into his interior office. Lisette followed him, carrying one of the papers.

"You're right, in that it has to be related. I'm just waiting for the police to arrest me for this one as well."

"Now, now, let's not be so pessimistic, Miss Darling. Did our private investigator friend offer any more help last night?"

Lisette had told Herbie about going to dinner with Byron. If anything, he'd been worse than Darcy about what that meant.

"We talked with Leroy, the trumpet player. He was pretty cryptic about things. He seems to know about something in her past, but he wouldn't tell us what it was. Something about a code. He indicated he might have the same thing in his past."

"What do you suppose that means?"

"It has to be something criminal. Byron suggested Verity may have invited me because of my own past, how close I was to murder as well."

Herbie sat back in thought.

"Do you suspect the same thing?" Lisette had been hoping Herbie would immediately dismiss the idea.

"It is something to consider. Having been so close to a prior murder investigation, it very much suits her purposes, if that was her plan all along. From what you told me about the masks and the change of dress, I wouldn't put it past Miss Vance to have it in mind to make people think it was you who murdered Troy."

"Which is exactly what I said yesterday, all with you telling me I was overreacting."

"Now, now, I still think it's a bit far-fetched, and it won't reach the point of going all the way to trial. Besides, with this latest unfortunate event, I do believe we may get closer to the truth."

"How so?"

"I'm certain Miss Ford may have pressed her luck with regard to the original murder. I assume, like the others, she was courted by Franklin Winthorpe. Perhaps she wasn't satisfied with his offer, or perhaps she found her conscience and decided to tell what she witnessed."

"From what little I've seen of her, I suspect the former." Lisette felt a twinge of self-reproach, speaking so frankly about the dead. She supposed if it helped bring Bethany's killer to justice, she wouldn't mind.

"Well then, perhaps she was murdered to silence her. She was either going to reveal that Franklin had been making the rounds among the witnesses, or that Verity was the murderer."

"So, other than Franklin, we should look at anyone who may have wanted to keep Verity's secret." Lisette thought about it. "The only one who might have cared is Neville. He may have been involved in whatever happened back in Louisiana, which Leroy was so cryptic about. I suppose that would include Cynthia as well. They're even less likely to talk to me if that's the case."

"Then you should look at who might have known what Bethany had in mind."

"Patricia," Lisette said almost instantly. "I could tell she wanted to talk when we were all gathering our things. With Bethany there, she was pressured into silence."

"Sadly, that shouldn't be a problem now."

"Yes, I just have to find her. We can look up Patricia Cresswell and hope she answers the phone, if she even has her own phone."

"Cresswell? As in Cresswell crackers?"

Lisette stared at Herbie, allowing that question to fall into place in her head. "Of course! That explains so much. Bethany made an offhand remark in our cabin, which I didn't pay too much attention to. That, and the pampered princess remarks." Lisette coughed out a laugh. "Of course she's part of *that* Cresswell family. That also means she'd have nothing that Franklin could offer to make her silent on the issue of Verity's guilt."

"Well, I can tell you they have a very impressive mansion in Beverly Hills."

"Of course they do. That city seems to be an underlying theme in this case. Even if she has her own residence somewhere, she's probably sequestered there if only to avoid the press. Which will make it near impossible to get to her."

"Yes, the wealthy do have a tendency to entrench themselves, especially when scandal is at hand. That poor girl probably won't see the light of day for the next few weeks, perhaps not until the trial is over."

"True," Lisette said with a sigh, falling back in the chair across from Herbie. "It's too bad, as she could probably single-handedly help us solve both murders. Even the police would be barred access to her by now, since her parents probably already have a team of lawyers serving as an obstacle. I almost feel sorry for her. She probably wasn't looking for this much excitement in her life."

Lisette sat up slowly as a dawning idea came to her.

"I know that look. What is it, my dear?"

Her mouth hitched up on one side. "I'm thinking of something quite scandalous, Herbie. I know how to draw Patricia out."

CHAPTER TWENTY-THREE

"It's not a bad plan. I'm almost mad I didn't think of it myself," Byron said when Lisette approached him with the idea she had to draw Patricia out from the clutches of her family and lawyers. He grinned at her. "Almost reminds me of how we first met."

Lisette smirked. "Which only goes to prove it might work."

"Well, then, we should move fast, before the press is on to the next Hollywood scandal."

An hour later, Lisette and Byron were in a truck. He was out of his suit and changed into workman's clothing, clean but casual. Lisette had come with him but would remain in the truck, as Patricia knew what she looked like. Still, she couldn't miss out on watching her brilliant plan play out—at least she hoped it was brilliant. It could backfire and have Patricia even more sheltered than before.

The Cresswells lived in the sort of Beverly Hills mansion fit for the family of a cracker empire. It was well ensconced, set far back from the street by a sturdy front gate. Fortunately for Lisette and Byron, there was a group of press gathered outside, hoping to get just a word from the young woman who had most likely witnessed one murder, and was quite close with the victim of another. All the better that she came from a wealthy family.

Byron parked the truck further down the road such that Lisette couldn't be seen, but she was close enough to hear and could watch everything unfold in the rearview mirror.

Byron got out and went around to the back of the truck. A moment later, Lisette saw him walking toward the front gate with a bouquet of flowers in his hands. The press looked on with curious expressions.

He pressed the intercom, and a moment later a voice sounded through it. *"The Cresswell family is not speaking with any press or making any statement. If you continue to—"*

"Yeah, uh, I got a bouquet of flowers here for a Miss Patricia Cresswell." Lisette was impressed by the subtle change in his voice, tone, and accent.

There was a pause before the voice, not Patricia's, spoke up again through the intercom. *"I beg your pardon?"*

"Flowers. For a Patricia Cresswell."

"We aren't accepting any flowers. Please take them back."

"Listen, ma'am, I have to deliver these or I don't get paid. I can leave 'em at the front gate here but they might get stolen by one of these people out here. If I was her, I maybe wouldn't want them reading what's on the inside of the small envelope attached. Say, what's going on with all these people, by the way?"

"Never mind them. I said we won't be accepting the flowers. Please take them back."

"I need Patricia to come and sign to refuse delivery for me to do that ma'am. Otherwise, she's got a bouquet sitting out here at the front gate. I have to assume her beau ain't gonna like other people reading whatever it is he wrote to her."

"*Who sent you?*" This was the voice of another woman, also not Patricia. The authoritative tone and note of suspicion meant it was probably her mother.

"They don't tell me these things, ma'am. I'm just the guy who delivers them. All I have here on my sheet is that they are from a Mr. Johnson." Lisette felt using Leroy's last name would be enough to stir Patricia into action, but it was also common enough that none of the press would figure out who he was. "Do you want me to open the envelope and read what it—"

"*No, don't do that, for heaven's sake.*" There was a pause before she spoke again. "*I'll send out someone to collect them. You just wait right there.*"

Lisette breathed out a sigh of relief. Part one of her plan had worked. She could see the press begin to buzz about, now asking Byron about the flowers and this Mr. Johnson he had mentioned. He simply stood there, ignoring them while a woman in a black maid's uniform hurried out. She didn't bother opening the gate. She simply reached through to sign for the flowers and then hastily took hold of them before rushing back into the house.

Byron continued to ignore the press as he jogged back to the truck. Blessedly, they weren't curious enough to follow him with their questions. One glimpse of Lisette might spark even more questions, as at least one of them would have recognized her.

"Now, we wait," Byron said with a grin.

"Let's hope this worked."

"It may, whether it gives us any useful information is the question."

"Crackers! I was supposed to ask Lucy about who it was Franklin sent to get the reels of Verity's movies today."

Byron smiled. "It's still morning, Lisette, it isn't as though she's left for the day. Come on, I'll drive you back to Olympus and we can do that while we wait to see if your plan pans out."

By the time they made it back to the studio lot and Lucy's archival hub, she was already in demand. Still, she met Lisette and Byron with a cheerful smile, as busy was her favorite mode to be in.

"Good morning, Lucy, I just need a brief bit of information from you."

"That is my role here at Olympus," she said with a small laugh. "How can I help you?"

"I just have a quick question. Franklin sent someone over to get the reels of movies Verity Vance had any small part in. Do you remember that?"

"Only now that I know it was regarding her. It was someone from Winthorpe Film, a reputable enough company to entrust our reels to. They simply had a list of movies they wanted to borrow. I had no idea what it was for."

Lisette was disappointed to learn that it had been a subsidiary of Winthorpe Media that had asked for the film. Franklin would have already instructed anyone involved not to speak with anyone, especially her. They'd never get their hands on that reel.

"Did you want to borrow those reels?"

"Not now, Lucy." She thought of something else. "Have

you completed your dossier on Verity Vance? I'd like to take a look, if so."

"You and everyone else," Lucy said with a laugh. "Even our carbon copies are checked out. One day someone will make a machine that easily reproduces copies or photographs with a simple push of the button. Until then, I'm afraid you'll have to wait."

Another disappointment. But waiting seemed to be the theme of the day.

A page rushed in with a request so Byron and Lisette left, allowing Lucy to get on with her job.

"Here's hoping Patricia has something helpful to tell us."

At nine o'clock that night, Byron and Lisette were back in the Satin Club listening to mellow jazz music once again. If anything, Tuesday was even more dead than Monday had been. That worked extremely well for their purposes.

Perhaps Patricia knew this as well because only a few minutes past the top of the hour, she arrived. Her eyes scanned the room, eventually alighting on Byron. She had probably been watching the show earlier that day from a window at the Cresswell residence. The spark of recognition when those eyes landed on Lisette was laced with panic.

Lisette was prepared to chase her down should she flee, but to her credit, she strutted right over to their table.

"Just what game are you two playing? You nearly got me sent to a convent."

"I thought we were fairly subtle. We had no intention of getting you into trouble, Patti."

She glared back at Lisette as she looked around nervously, then took a seat. "'Be in satin at nine?' Thank goodness my parents don't know about this place. They aren't stupid, you know. It was all I could do to feign a stomach ache and sneak out. I felt like I was sixteen again."

Lisette smiled at the idea Patricia was far more rebellious than she'd originally given her credit for. "Hasn't that always been the reason why you came here?"

Patricia's lips tightened with irritation. "What do you want?"

"You know what I want."

"I didn't see Verity shoot Troy."

"Patti," Lisette felt her impatience grow.

"No, really, I didn't. Betts and I—" She swallowed hard, choking up at the mention of Bethany. "We were doing some silly routine. Yes, I saw Verity and Troy having a heated conversation just before she stormed out. Betts ramped up the dancing, getting the jazz band to get a bit louder so no one would notice when she returned."

"Do you think she knew what was about to happen? That Verity was going to get her gun?" Lisette was shocked that this might be the case.

Patricia shook her head. "I don't think so. She screamed the loudest when the shot rang out. I think she just didn't want people to see Verity go into one of her tantrums. Betts really wanted to get on her good side, if it meant getting better roles and becoming a star." The mention of her name had Patricia in tears now. Byron reached into his pocket for a handkerchief to hand to her.

"I'm so sorry about Betts, Patti."

"You should be ashamed of yourself," she said, before wiping her eyes and nose. "Playing such a dirty trick after what happened to her."

"Yes, it was a bit underhanded," Lisette confessed. "But we may find out who killed her if we can learn Verity's motive for killing Troy."

"Why would they be related?"

"You know Franklin has been trying to silence everyone, even Bethany. It was obvious she was keeping you from talking back on the boat. Did he get to you too?"

"With what? I don't want to be a star or famous or anything like that. I just liked having a bit of fun."

"But Bethany did want all that. Maybe she wanted more than he was willing to give?"

"I suppose we'll never know now, will we?" Patricia gave her a scolding look as though it was her fault she was dead.

Lisette decided to keep pressing Patricia while she had her. "Is Verity trying to eventually frame me?"

Patricia's eyes above the handkerchief were touched with guilt. "I don't know. Though...I had considered it."

Lisette felt a rush of satisfaction at having her suspicions confirmed and righteous anger at the idea they might be true. "Was that her plan all along? Is that why she invited me and brought the gun?"

"Verity always carries a gun. It was her thing. She told me that back home—" Patricia stopped, her eyes going wide with guilt.

"Oh for heaven's sake, Patti, there's no point in protecting her now."

Patricia exhaled and dropped the handkerchief from her face. "She let it slip once that she was from Louisiana. She said the first thing she did before coming to California was to get rid of her accent and change her name. Then, one of the first things she did once she got here was get a gun. Said she wasn't allowed to have one back home. I'm

179

guessing her parents were pretty strict about that; she never really talks about them. Verity always liked to do things she wasn't allowed to. It was as though she saw every 'no' as a challenge. That's how she met Franklin in the first place. He was in the exclusive section of a club and she just sashayed her way there when no one was looking and walked right up to him. I guess he liked that."

"So you weren't surprised to find she had brought a gun on board the yacht?"

"I would have been surprised if she *hadn't* brought it with her."

Lisette glanced at Byron. He lifted his brow with the same thought. They were back to the murder possibly not being premeditated.

"Did Verity say anything after you took her to her cabin? Anything that might indicate why she'd shot him."

"I said I didn't see her shoot him," Patricia insisted, a petulant look in her eyes.

"Who else might it have been?" Lisette's voice had an exaggerated note of politeness, as though Patricia's insistence on suggesting Verity hadn't been the shooter was bordering on the insane.

"I'm just saying...in case someone wants to put me on the stand. My parents would kill me."

"We're not here for that."

"Why don't we start at the beginning," Byron said, leaning in with that disarming smile of his. He gently placed a hand on top of Patricia's. "How did you and Verity meet?"

"That was all Betts. She came here every so often and we just started talking. She was the one to introduce me to Verity about a year ago. She'd met her at some other club."

"So you've known her for a year. Obviously, you two hit it off. She invited you to her birthday party."

"Verity invited Betts. Betts invited me. She wanted this black and white theme and Betts thought it would be a hoot to have the jazz band come on board to play. I thought for sure Verity would say no, but she loved the idea of a jazz band. Odd, since she hated this place the one time we brought her. At any rate, I told the gal organizing her party to hire the guys that usually play here. They're all nice fellas. "

"Why didn't she like this place?"

"Verity liked it swanky, is all. Only the best for her. She preferred places like Montmartre or the Cocoanut Grove, if she could ever get in. Franklin certainly helped with that."

"Betts mentioned knowing where all the bodies were buried. Do you know what she meant by that?"

"She was just saying that. She liked to play that way, make people focus on her by being provocative. The truth is, I don't think anyone really knew anything about Verity."

"You knew she changed her name," Byron hinted.

"Yes, but that's no big secret. No one is really named Verity Vance."

"Wait..." Lisette paused, reversing the conversation in her head. "You said Verity changed her name back in Louisiana, *before* coming to California?"

"That's what she told us."

Lisette turned to Byron, who, based on his expression, just had the same thought. She turned back to Patricia. "So you knew she was Marie LeBlanc before she became Verity."

Patricia nodded.

"Lennie told us she came to him for advice on changing

her name. That was back when she was still Marie LeBlanc."

"Which means she changed her name twice," Byron said, one side of his mouth hitched up as he turned to Lisette. "So, who was she before she became Marie LeBlanc?"

CHAPTER TWENTY-FOUR

LISETTE AND BYRON had thanked Patricia, who was more than happy to leave them at the Satin Club. The two of them finished the drinks they had ordered and Byron drove Lisette home. On the way, they discussed what Patricia had revealed in relation to Troy's murder.

"I think if we find out who she was before she became Marie LeBlanc, we may find out what she was trying to hide."

"Even then, we still have to find out how Troy knew. That's the key."

"It's something on that reel. Oh, I could kick myself for taking a nap while it was being shown!"

"I doubt that would have changed anything. It seems Troy was the only one to pick up on something from the films."

"In which case, it's essentially like having a coded message but with no key to decrypt it."

"Perhaps, but I believe we can at least narrow things down."

"How?"

"Let's look at the name Marie LeBlanc. We now know that's what she changed it to in Louisiana, before coming to California. It's rather French, don't you think?"

"Yes, but that makes sense. She was in Louisiana, after all," Lisette pointed out. "Maybe that name is as common as Marie Smith down there."

"Yes, but once she came to California, she suddenly seemed to want to rid herself of anything that might reveal where she's from. Losing her accent was understandable. I doubt it would have helped her land any roles. Perhaps her original name was too eccentric to be marketable. Then, once she was here, she never talked about her parents, and according to Patricia, only once let it slip that she was from Louisiana. I thought it rather interesting she phrased it that way, as though Verity may have regretted it at the time, or perhaps even warned her not to tell anyone."

"So, once again we're back to her roots."

"Let me ask you something."

"Go on."

"The name Marie LeBlanc. I happen to think it's rather nice, memorable even. Perfectly marketable. Verity Vance seems a bit...vaudeville. I know comedy was her forte, as Lennie claimed, but it limits her range. What if she decided to go into serious roles?"

Lisette smirked. "I suppose she could just change it again. That also seems to be her forte. Perhaps next time she'll get advice from Clark Gable, he's done pretty well in both comedy and drama. She might as well go back to Marie LeBlanc. You're right, it isn't such a bad name, and she certainly has range as far as acting goes. She sure had everyone fooled this past weekend. I had no idea she was a murderer," Lisette said, her mouth twisting with resentment.

"Focus, Darling. It's the timing I'm thinking of. Somewhere in between arriving in California and meeting Lennie Lamar, she decided to become Verity Vance."

Lisette thought about it. "He said it was on one of her earliest films that he met her. If only that filmography Lucy created had been available. I suppose we can check tomorrow."

"Yes, if we get a hold of those first films, we may find out what it was Troy saw. At the very least, we can talk to people who worked on the films, see if anything happened during filming that might give us a clue."

They arrived at Lisette's small apartment building. Byron walked her to the front door, but before they even reached the walkway leading to it, they heard Darcy calling from the window.

"Lisette! I've been waiting all night for you! Did you hear the latest news on the radio?"

Lisette and Byron both craned their necks, looking up to the window her roommate was practically falling out of.

"Goodness, Darcy, get back inside. We're coming up," Lisette said, knowing the neighbors would be having a fit at the commotion.

"But it's Lennie Lamar!" Darcy continued, completely ignoring her. "He's been arrested!"

That had Lisette and Byron staring at each other, eyes wide. Lisette quickly opened the front door of the building and they rushed up to her apartment. Darcy already had the door open, leaning against the frame with a cat-that-ate-the-canary grin on her face.

"Hi-ya Byron. Another 'working' dinner tonight?"

"Darcy," Lisette said, exasperated. "Why was Lennie arrested?"

"Oh, yes!" She quickly rushed back into the living room

and fell onto the couch. Lisette took the space next to her and Byron remained standing. "Bethany Ford, the one who was just found? Lennie turned himself in for murdering her."

"Wait, he turned himself in?" Lisette was surprised.

"Yep. Claims it was self-defense. And that's not all!"

Lisette was about to burst with frustration at Darcy making them draw each bit of information out of her.

"What else is there?" Byron asked with just the right amount of patience and eagerness to appease Darcy.

"He claims *she* also killed Troy Turner!" The excitement with which Darcy revealed this information was jarringly incongruous with the information imparted.

"What?" Lisette nearly shot up from the couch in surprise. "He didn't!"

"He did!"

"You heard all of this on the radio?" Byron said, a note of skepticism in his voice.

"Yes," Darcy insisted, pouting a bit. "Well, they said that there was some *suspicion* that Bethany *may have* shot Troy. It seems the police aren't fully convinced. But the part about Lennie claiming she came to him with a gun, that's all true!"

"So he says," Lisette muttered. She bit her thumb in thought. She should have been relieved. Both murders were seemingly solved. Still, something about it seemed off. She glanced up at Byron. He stared back, the expression on his face indicating he had his doubts as well.

"Bethany certainly didn't kill Troy, though I don't know who from that trip will come forward and say as much. I also doubt she came after Lennie the way he claims. Why would she?"

"You had the same question about Verity and Troy," Darcy pointed out. "Why would *she* have killed him?"

"But we know there's an answer lurking out there somewhere. Everyone keeps alluding to it, we just have to pull back the curtain on it."

"So Lennie is taking the fall for someone then," Byron said. "We know it isn't Verity as she was still in custody when Bethany was murdered. Then again, he could have just killed her to silence her."

"I think it still boils down to Bethany either telling the truth about Verity killing Troy or wanting more than what Franklin was offering."

"Both of which boil down to Bethany being a threat to Verity," Byron said. "Someone wanted to silence Bethany."

"Or perhaps got angry enough to go too far during a heated argument with her."

"Oh, what if Verity had a coconspirator on the boat?" Darcy interjected. "It could be Franklin, or maybe even Bethany! I read a story in a magazine about two men conspiring to kill someone but only one got caught. There was no evidence for the other, so he—"

"I think, we should probably focus on the two crimes we're already dealing with."

"But you are getting somewhere with that, Darcy," Byron said before he began pacing.

"I am?"

"She is?"

Both women stared at Byron in surprise as he continued to pace, his finger to his chin in thought.

"Not a coconspirator, but someone else with something to lose if Verity's secret got out." He stopped and stared at them. "Perhaps Lennie isn't protecting Verity. Maybe he's protecting himself."

"You think whatever Troy discovered affects him as well? That he killed Bethany to keep her from revealing it?"

"Perhaps. It's either that, or the man is truly a fool in love, as you said. I've seen it before, back when I was working in San Francisco. People under that spell do crazy things, *evil* things. He may very well be sitting in a cell regretting everything now that he's had time to cool his head."

"Either way, I think we know exactly which film to start with tomorrow," Lisette said, feeling her anticipation grow to ravenous levels, wondering what they would discover.

CHAPTER TWENTY-FIVE

LISETTE HARDLY SLEPT, she was so eager to see Verity's film history and find out exactly which one led her to Lennie. She settled herself with the knowledge that at least the police wouldn't be focusing on her as she'd feared might be the case. Lennie had shifted all the attention to himself.

Lisette had insisted Byron handle his own business, as this was nothing more than an errand. After all, he had bills to pay. She knew Lucy arrived at eight on the dot. Short of the Huxleys themselves, everyone had to wait until then if they needed information from her archives. In all fairness, there was rarely an information emergency.

By the time eight hit, Lisette was waiting outside the building trying to keep her toe from tapping with impatience.

When Lucy arrived, she pursed her lips. "I suppose I shouldn't be surprised to see you. Three times in as many days, Lisette. People will begin to wonder if you've traded bosses."

"Herbie would be devastated," Lisette said with a laugh as she followed her in.

"Lucky you, you are first in line for Verity's file today. Or are we pulling Lennie's again? Such startling news that came in last night. I've already sent James and Agatha out to collect every newspaper and get copies of any public information available from the police department."

"Naturally."

"Do you think he's telling the truth, that Bethany Ford tried to kill him just as she did Troy?"

"I suppose that's for a jury to decide," Lisette responded judiciously.

Lucy pursed her lips again, this time with irritation.

"Lucy," Lisette admonished. "Don't you deal in facts and facts alone?"

That earned her a laugh. "I suppose that depends on whether you consider the news factual. Certainly, Hedley put her little spin on things. I dutifully included it in Verity's file all the same. Speaking of which, is it just Verity today?"

"For now. I only need the list of films she's been in." Lisette was familiar with all of Lennie's work and hoped she'd be able to spot the film they were both in without Lucy having to get his information as well.

Lucy disappeared and quickly came back with it. "Here's the list, all in reverse chronological order, complete with character or part, director, and studio."

"God bless you, Lucy," Lisette said, her eyes already on the list that she instantly dragged closer.

She started at the bottom, where Verity's parts were nothing more than "Maid #1" or "Girl in audience." Her eyes came to a sudden stop at *Last Laugh*. That was a Lennie Lamar movie, not his best work, despite the title. It started with a bang on release day, then fizzled when audiences were less than impressed with it. Lisette saw that Verity's role was "Cigarette girl." The role must have been tiny, as Lisette didn't remember her in it, not that she remembered much about the underwhelming film. Still, she vaguely remembered a club scene, which was the only short part of the movie where a cigarette girl would be placed.

One interesting thing she noted was that it had been made in 1933 when Verity would have only been sixteen or seventeen. Perhaps that was the scandal? Lennie Lamar and an underage girl? But usually, men with such a vice made it into a bad habit. Lisette hadn't heard anything like that about him, even through the grapevine. Besides, he'd hardly be the first man to stoop so low, so it wasn't a career killer. Which meant, it had to be something either on that specific film or something Troy had learned about the production of it.

"Find anything interesting?"

"Yes, I found what I was—" She stopped when her eyes landed on the studio that had produced the film: Empire. Lisette's eyes flashed up to Lucy. "It's an Empire film."

"What is?" Lucy couldn't mask the avid curiosity in her voice.

"*Last Laugh*, it's gone. This film was from two years ago."

"Oh, oh dear. Yes, that means it would have been lost in the fire most likely."

"Then how did Franklin get a copy?" To be fair, Lisette still wasn't sure this was the film that had set Troy off, but at this point, it was far too much of a coincidence not to be.

"Not all copies were lost. Sometimes directors, producers, or even actors request copies of their films for a personal collection. Lenora, my counterpart that they hired after the fact, had a heck of a time scrounging up as many as she could find. It was like a treasure hunt, really. I imagine it was as fun as it was frustrating." Lucy sighed, as though wishing she had been lucky enough to be involved in such an undertaking.

Lisette thought of the director, Eddie Carmichael. He hadn't worked on a film in over a year and a half. In fact, *Last Laugh* was one of the last in a string of films that had done poorly at the box office. Would he have held onto one of the films that put the final nail in his occupational coffin? Lisette wasn't sure...but she knew someone who *would* have wanted a personal copy. The same man who had taken quite a personal interest in Verity and her career. The same man who was at the moment not only on the road to perjuring himself but perhaps even going to prison for her.

"Thank you, Lucy," Lisette said, rushing out.

"What is it you were looking for?" Lucy called out after her.

"You'll read it in the papers," Lisette shouted back, unable to contain a small smile on her face. She wasn't about to feed the gossip mill by telling Lucy what she'd been in search of.

Not until she got her hands on that film.

The only problem was, how to access it. She had an idea, one she wasn't particularly fond of. She reassured herself it was for the sake of justice.

Half an hour later she was at the Hollywood division of the LAPD. She was happy to see that there was no press outside. Granted, West Hollywood, Beverly Hills, and Hollywood all had different jurisdictions. Even Troy's murder wouldn't have been handled by this station house.

Lisette was a well-known figure in the Hollywood division of the LAPD, though feelings were mixed about whether her presence was a positive or negative thing. Still, as always, eyes followed her all the way to Detective Mason Sharkey's desk. This was the main reason she had decided not to bring Byron in on this little jaunt. No need for pride and jealousy to interfere with her mission.

Mason's expression no longer bore the signs of hopeful longing at her appearance. Lisette had gone out with him for several months before calling things off. She'd seen a side of him she didn't particularly approve of. His feelings for her had lasted longer than she would have liked, but she was glad they seemed to have waned by now.

"I don't know why you're here. The Sheriff's Department has Lennie. West Hollywood is in the county's jurisdiction, not LAPD's."

"I see you can read my mind these days," she replied with a wry smile as she took the seat at his desk.

"Don't get comfortable, I have no information for you. We aren't going anywhere near this case. It's almost as messy as the Turner murder."

"Oh?"

His expression told her he wasn't fooled by the innocent look of curiosity.

"I actually came because I don't think Lennie killed Bethany, at least not for the reasons stated. I think there's a lot more going on in both cases, which I believe are related. Again, not for the reasons Lennie has given."

"All of which you can pass on to the Sheriff's Department, or the Beverly Hills P.D."

"Why the dispute?" Lisette had an inkling, but she wanted to get him talking.

"Because if Miss Ford was killed at his home, which he

claims, that's Beverly Hills. But the body was found in West Hollywood, which is LA County."

"I see, so, who would have conducted the search of his home? Surely that's standard procedure in a murder investigation?"

He studied her with a patient, humorless smile. "Why don't you tell me what you're really after, Lisette?"

"I should have known I couldn't fool you."

"Flattery won't work either. I'd prefer it if you were straight with me."

Lisette exhaled and nodded. "Fair enough. This idea that Bethany killed Troy is laughable. As is the idea that she threatened Lennie to the point he needed to kill her in self-defense. Have you seen the size of him? Perhaps he did kill her but if he did it was to keep Verity's secret, the same reason she killed Troy Turner."

Through her entire assertion, Mason sat back in his chair with a subtle smile on his face.

"What is it?"

"I probably shouldn't even tell you but...they found the gun used to kill Troy Turner with Miss Ford's body. The bullets in the gun match the one they found in Turner's body."

"*What?*"

Detective Sharkey shrugged. "That kind of paints things with Mr. Lamar's brush, not yours. Either he already had possession of the gun himself or Bethany brought it over to threaten him with as he claims."

"Are you telling me, the police searched that ship—my luggage included, I might add—and still didn't find the gun that killed Troy?"

Again Detective Sharkey shrugged. "I suppose they

figured it was swimming with the fishes. Now, we know either Bethany Ford or Lennie Lamar took it off the ship."

"Oh, she's good," Lisette murmured, surprised to find herself admiring Verity's ingenuity. "I suppose this also paints things in a way that makes Verity look even more innocent."

"That's for a jury to decide. I'm sure any good lawyer will bring up the gun being involved in a subsequent murder, all while she was conveniently still in custody."

"But where—" Lisette stopped when she considered something. "I think Franklin and Verity had a secret passageway or something between their rooms. Did the police find it? That's where the gun could have been hidden."

For the first time, Detective Sharkey seemed intrigued. He sat up and leaned in closer with a serious expression. "I can certainly tell them about it. How did you know about it?"

"Something Bethany mentioned when I first met her. I should point out that she, Verity, and Patti were holed up together right after the murder. I can verify that I saw Verity holding the gun, then she dropped it. After that, Franklin had everyone go to their respective cabins. So who was left guarding the body and the gun? When we finally returned to get our things, Bethany and Patricia boarded before me, they also left after me. That would have given Bethany plenty of opportunity to quickly get the gun and put it in her belongings. The only police presence by then was stationed right at the gangplank to keep the press out."

Mason coughed out a silent, bitter laugh and shook his head. "Amateurs. This is what happens when they're too busy fighting over who gets the case."

"Just as with this second murder. Why else would Lennie have left Bethany's body in another city, one that doesn't even have its own police department? It was all to make a mess of the jurisdiction so his legal team can get all their ducks in a row while the authorities are battling it out. Who knows what audacious story they're crafting as we speak?"

"Let's not jump to conclusions."

"What was his excuse for moving her body?"

"He claims he originally didn't want the publicity. He is Lennie Lamar, after all. Then, a bout of guilt hit him and he turned himself in. Technically, moving the body was another crime altogether."

"Exactly."

Detective Mason released a heavy breath, as though he didn't envy the other departments. "Again, not my mess. Did I give you the answers you were here for? Because we both know this wasn't a social call."

"I'm only trying to help find the real killer, Mason. Don't you think there's something fishy about all of this?"

"Yes, but I also think it's not my jurisdiction, and it certainly isn't yours."

"Some people had the idea that Verity would be using me to take the fall. We do look alike." Lisette gave him a moment to study her and confirm that fact. "Perhaps someone got spooked by the idea I wouldn't be such easy prey and decided on a different path, like blaming Bethany?"

"Not such easy prey, huh? And why would they think that? Have you been meddling in this case?"

"I prefer to think of it as self-preservation."

"Lisette."

She ignored his warning tone. "Never mind that. What

I really need is access to a reel of *Last Laugh*. I think there might be a clue there."

"And you think we have a secret stash of film reels held here at the department?" He coughed out a laugh.

"No," she said with a droll smile. "But I'm sure Lennie has a copy. It was produced by Empire and they had that fire a while back…. Say, was the cause of that fire ever determined?"

"A lit match. Maybe foul play, maybe from some idiot lighting a cigarette. You'd have thought there would be a no smoking policy around movie film."

"I'd bet there was." Lisette gave him a meaningful look.

"Oh no you don't. That's another area well outside of your jurisdiction."

"Unless it's related."

"And if it is, then—oh, hell, I don't even know why I bother anymore. It's obvious you're going to do what you usually do and interfere."

"For the sake of justice."

"Yeah, yeah."

"Don't be so pessimistic, Detective Sharkey. I'll be sure to credit you if I manage to solve all three cases."

"Please don't. I wouldn't touch any of this with a sixty-foot pole. You would think such an open and shut case to begin with would be easy and done."

"Yes, I suppose that's why Verity made it complicated, her and whoever is helping her, inadvertently or deliberately."

"At least try not to get yourself killed as well."

"I'll do my best, detective." Lisette smiled and rose to leave. She had learned far more than she'd come for. She was sure it was Bethany who had gotten that gun off the boat. Either that, or the person who was trying to frame her for Troy's murder. Right now, that person was still Lennie Lamar.

Now, Lisette wanted to see that reel more than ever. Even if Lennie had a copy, it would be near impossible to get via him. She bit her thumb as she sat in the car to ponder it. In the end, she realized, she had nothing to run on but hope and luck. She started the car to pursue it.

CHAPTER TWENTY-SIX

LISETTE QUICKLY DROVE to Byron's office. Her eagerness to include him in her next step of the case was thwarted by the appearance of his secretary...and a waiting room that actually had paying clients inside.

"Miss Darling is it?" Roberta greeted with a polite, professional smile.

"I—yes, that's correct. I suppose we haven't been officially introduced, Mrs...?"

Roberta seemed pleasantly taken aback but obliged. "Mrs. Garfield."

"Yes, Mrs. Garfield. I'm sorry, I didn't mean to—"

Lisette was already turning to leave when Byron's door opened and a woman, presumably a client, walked out to leave. "Why Miss Darling, what a pleasant surprise." The look on his face indicated he had expected her long before now.

"I don't want to take you away from your paying clients," she said, casting a quick look toward his waiting room and then back to him.

"Yes, this is a business," he said with a heavy sigh, then

brightened up. "But I'm curious, all the same." He turned to the waiting room. "My apologies, ladies and gentlemen, it will be five more minutes, ten at the most."

Mrs. Garfield didn't seem pleased by that, but Byron whisked Lisette into his office and closed the door all the same. He took a seat behind his desk and Lisette sat across from him.

"So what have you been up to since we last met? Did you manage to get a hold of the film?"

"That's proving to be far more difficult than I thought. The film Lennie and Verity were both in was *Last Laugh*, and it was an Empire Studios release. The studio whose warehouse of film burned down almost two years ago? Very conveniently, I'd say."

"Very."

"But even more interesting is that I learned the gun used to shoot Troy was found with Bethany's body."

He leaned in with interest. "How very intriguing."

"Very."

Lisette told him everything she had learned from Detective Sharkey.

"It certainly helps to support Lennie's supposed claim that Bethany was the one to shoot Troy."

"She doesn't deserve that, whatever her actions were after the fact. Patti even stated they were dancing together at the same time."

"She also said Bethany was attempting to distract everyone for Verity's sake."

"Do you think she was in on it?"

Byron considered it. "From everything you've told me, I think Bethany was an opportunist. Whether that had her working with Verity beforehand or after the fact is the question. One which may never be answered. I also don't see her threatening someone with a gun, not when she had so much more effective ammunition. Information is power, after all."

"Agreed."

"So what are you going to do now?"

Lisette had been hoping Byron would join her, but she didn't want to take him from jobs that would actually pay the bills. He grinned as though reading her mind.

"I have complete faith in you, Lisette. In case you hadn't noticed, you've been handling this case mostly by yourself. I'd be worried about the competition if I didn't know your ambitions lay elsewhere."

Her mouth twisted into a reluctant smile of pleasure. "I plan on talking to Eddie Carmichael, the director. I think he might be able to shed some light on what it was Troy must have discovered. With any luck, perhaps he even has a copy of *Last Laugh*."

"Smart girl."

"No need to patronize me."

"Balderdash! It's exactly what I would have done. Now off with you Detective Darling. I have a feeling wheels are in motion to spin a narrative that may see justice thwarted. Time is of the essence. However, I insist on dinner this evening to learn all about it."

"You can just ask me out to dinner, you know?"

"What fun would that be?"

Lisette laughed and stood up. "Eight as usual?"

"On the dot."

She left feeling bolstered by Byron's confidence in her. She didn't know why. After all, she'd been doing similar work for Herbie for several years by now. It was almost old hat. Still, this was far more exciting than babysitting stars or trading favors with the press. She had to temper herself, remembering that two people were dead and she was on a mission to find out why.

Eddie Carmichael lived in a nice home in Malibu. By the standards of most Americans, he might as well have been Mr. Moneybags. By Hollywood standards, it was modest. Lisette had thought about calling ahead of time but decided that since she had the use of one of Olympus's cars, she might as well drive over. She didn't want to give him advance notice as to what she was after. Worst case scenario, he wouldn't be home.

However, Eddie was indeed home. Lisette supposed that was one of the benefits of not having any recent directing work. Perhaps he was enjoying an early retirement. He opened the door and Lissette saw what years of no work had done to him. He hadn't completely gone to rot, but he also hadn't bothered changing out of his pajamas, running a comb through his hair, or shaving by the middle of the day. At least he'd had the decency to put on a robe.

He studied Lisette, a hint of recognition in his eyes. "How do I know you?"

"I'm Lisette Darling, I work at Olympus Studios for Herbie—"

"Hinkle," he finished with a crooked grin. "How is old Herbie these days? One of the few people in Hollywood that isn't a complete—" He stopped himself, giving Lisette a wary look as though she might go tattling on him. "What did you want, honey?"

"I wanted to discuss one of your films, *Last Laugh*."

The look of disgust that instantly came to his face was impossible to miss. "I have no interest in being reminded of that disaster. And when I think about what that film coulda been..." He shook his head in disappointment.

"That's what I'd like to talk to you about. Do you mind if I come in?"

He studied her again, this time with a tinge of suspicion. His mouth hitched on one side and he shrugged. "Come on in, sweetheart."

Lisette ignored the pet name and entered, reminding herself it was all for a good cause. Or at least for justice.

"You want a drink or something? I've got whiskey and whiskey." He chuckled to himself.

"No, thank you."

"You don't mind if I do."

She didn't bother responding, as it wasn't a question. It was obvious he'd already had a few. She felt a bit of empathy hit her. It wasn't easy making it in Hollywood, and it was probably just as hard coming back from failure. She took a chair in the den that he led her to, while he poured himself a drink.

"Now then, how shall I entertain thee with the last laugh that was *Last Laugh*?"

"Do you happen to have a personal copy of the film?"

He grunted out a laugh. "Why would I keep a copy of that bad luck charm on hand?"

She felt her disappointment set in, even though she had mostly expected as much. "Then, can you tell me anything about a woman named Verity Vance? She might have been Marie LeBlanc at the time."

He paused, staring hard at her for so long, she thought he might eventually erupt, sending her packing. Instead, he seemed to sober up long enough to reply in a low, measured tone.

"That woman is bad news."

Lisette's eyes widened in surprise at the statement. "How so?"

"The moment she was involved in the film it all started to go to hell. She had one dang word in the whole dang movie. 'Cigarettes?'" Eddie intoned in a sing-song voice, mimicking her in an exaggerated manner. He danced his way over to the couch across from her, his drink sloshing precariously in its glass, and plopped onto it.

"What sorts of problems did she cause?"

"What problems *didn't* she cause? I should have known, as soon as Lennie mentioned her by name, she'd be a problem. Who pays attention to the extras? Beyond just a little flirting or hanky-panky? I wouldn't have even known her name if not for Lennie. First, it was more screen time for her. Then, she wanted to say more than one word. Then, one of the performers in the band had to be replaced. Then, it was—"

"I'm sorry, did you say a performer in the band? A jazz band?" Lisette seemed to remember that from the film.

"Essentially, but obviously we couldn't call it as such, even in the pre-code days. The joint in the film was meant to be seedy, but not that seedy. We didn't want to turn people off to it."

"And she wanted a band member removed?"

"Some saxophone player. This came from Lennie, not her, mind you. But I know who was pulling those strings. I'm pretty sure he paid the guy a small fortune out of his own funds to make him go quietly. The darn fella made more than he would have from being in the movie, so I'm sure he was happy to oblige. The only person attached to that stinker of a film who came out better for it."

"Did either of them give you a reason why they wanted him replaced?"

"When Lennie asks, I don't ask why. Besides, it wasn't as though I was handling those minor things. Still, it had a ripple effect. People got itchy, wondering what had happened, if they'd be next to go. Cinema is just as superstitious as the stage, sweetheart."

"So you're certain she was the cause of it? It couldn't have been some issue Lennie had with the man?"

"That woman—*Marie*." He spat her name out with contempt, then his mouth curled into a cruel smile. "Or I suppose she goes by Verity these days. Interesting choice of name for such a little chameleon, don't you think? Or perhaps I should call her a butterfly, the way she blossomed from that little caterpillar selling cigarettes."

That same thought had fleeted through Lisette's mind, though she hadn't been quite as cynical about it. Verity was a common enough name and worked well with Vance. Now, she wondered if there was some hidden meaning behind it.

"Were she and Lennie...involved with one another?"

He coughed out a laugh. "I don't think Lennie knew quite what to do with her. He was more like...an older brother. She had him playing the white knight like a puppet on a string. Good thing for him, because that girl definitely wasn't eighteen as she claimed." He snorted with derision. "I should have used that as an excuse to get her kicked off the film."

"Can you think of any reason why she wouldn't want that film shown in public?"

"Other than it being a big fat bust at the box office?" He gurgled a humorless laugh.

"Is there a possibility she might have been responsible for the fire that destroyed most of Empire Studios' films?"

He stared at Lisette with a considering look, as though that idea was falling into place in a specific part of his mind. "Does this have to do with her shooting Troy?"

"Yes," she said, feeling hopeful again. "Can you think of why she shot him?"

He slowly shook his head, his expression becoming somber. "I told the bastard not to put her on any of his films. Kiss of death, I said."

"Wait, you spoke to him before the trip? When was this?"

"After he got the invitation to that party. He figured it was all a ploy to get him to direct a film starring her. He came to me to learn more about her. Smart boy, does his research. I should have been as meticulous, but who knew back then what trouble she'd be?"

"What exactly did you say to him?"

"The same thing I told you. She's trouble, bad luck."

Lisette pondered that. Did Troy tell Verity he wouldn't be starring her in any of his films? That was hardly cause for her to kill him, especially with the time it took for her to decide on murder. She would have had to go to her cabin, get the gun, and then return to shoot him. Hardly a crime of passion. There had to be more to it than that.

"You looking to nail that little she-devil?" Eddie asked, pulling her out of her thoughts.

"I'm looking for a motive, something that would prove why she shot Troy. What you've told me so far won't cut it. Any good lawyer would shred it to pieces as far as motive. Plenty of starlets are turned down for parts. No, I think he saw something on that film that told him more, something that had her worried or offended enough to kill him."

Something flickered in his gaze, turning his eyes into flints. "I got your film."

"I'm sorry?"

"I said, I've got a copy of *Last Laugh*. 'Course I do. What director doesn't have copies of all their films, even the ones they wish they could burn to ashes? If it'll help you send that vixen to prison for good, you can have it."

"I just need to look at it," Lisette said, her heartbeat quickening.

"Well, come on then," he said, drunkenly getting to his feet. "Let's go look at it."

He had a small theater in his home, which wasn't a surprise, being a former director. Lisette kept her impatience in check as she followed Eddie's lazy stumble to that part of the house. She then watched with worry as he pulled out the reel and attempted to properly set it on his projector, slapping away her attempts to help. Lisette exhaled with relief when it was finally set, happy he hadn't destroyed the rare reel in the process.

"I just need the scene with Verity in it."

He sped the reel until just before Lennie's character entered the seedy club. There was Verity, looking pretty and oh so young and innocent in her sequined and satin one-piece costume.

"Cigarette?" she asked, her dimpled cheeks drawing the eye.

Lennie made some quippy remark meant to incur laughs, but Lisette had tuned him out in favor of the band playing in the background. They were meant to be part of the scenery, glossed over in favor of Lennie and his performance. But Lisette, like Troy most likely had been, was paying close attention to every detail in that scene.

And she had just discovered what it was Troy saw.

CHAPTER TWENTY-SEVEN

Lisette tried to control herself as she drove from Eddie's home. The last thing she wanted was to get into a crash just when she had found the very thing that might lead to an answer as to Verity's motive for killing Troy.

She realized she was heading to Byron's office rather than back to Olympus Studios. It was telling that the first person she wanted to share the news with was Byron rather than Herbie, which she certainly would have done even a few months ago.

She parked the car and rushed up the stairs to his office, breathless as she finally entered. There was no one in the waiting area at the moment, so she shot Roberta a huge grin and opened the door to his office, rushing in.

"Miss Darling!" Roberta called after her.

"I've found it! It was right there in the movie in black and white." She breathed out a quick laugh. "No wonder Troy was so subdued during dinner. He'd learned her secret, or was close to figuring it out. That's why she shot him! Leroy, that little sneak, he was right. The answer was right there on the yacht the whole time. Again, I could kick myself for sleeping through that darn screening. If I hadn't I would have—"

Lisette stopped, realizing that it wasn't just Byron staring at her with a mix of shock and amusement. She turned to see a finely dressed woman giving her an appalled look.

"Oh dear," she breathed out. "I...I'm so sorry, I thought you were alone."

"Miss Darling, I tried to tell you he was with a client," Roberta said in a censuring tone behind her.

Lisette felt her cheeks redden. "Again, I'm sorry. I'll come back—"

"Is this about the Troy Turner murder?" The woman said, her appalled look transforming into one of avid curiosity. "What is it you've discovered?"

"Miss Applebaum, perhaps we should focus on why you'd like to hire my services instead?"

She waved Byron's suggestion away with an irritated flip of the hand. "Nonsense, I'm here now. Go on, dear. What is it you've found out about the murder?"

"I...I really shouldn't say in front of—"

"You were quite eager to say so in front of Mr. Linley. Why not me? Is it really such a secret? Everyone is dying to know why that girl Bethany shot Troy Turner. I still think Verity had something to do with it all, even if they've allowed her out on bail now. But all the same, you've interrupted my consultation, so I'm using my time to learn the truth firsthand before anyone else."

Now, Lisette was the one appalled. She could understand Mrs. Applebaum's curiosity, but to be so blatant about it was rather tactless. Still, she couldn't contain the bubble of excitement that was ready to burst inside of her.

"He was right there on the film all along if you were paying attention, at any rate."

"What film?" This came from Mrs. Applebaum, earning her a look of irritation from Byron.

"*Last Laugh*."

"With Lennie Lamar? Awful film."

"Who was in the film?" Byron asked, leaning in to draw Lisette's attention.

"Leroy." Lisette refrained from using his last name, though she wasn't sure why, considering how much he had kept from her...and the police. "Verity had one of the band members removed from the film and replaced by someone else. Guess who else was in that band?"

"So he probably knew the man who was removed and the reasons why." Byron's eyes were just as lit with excitement as Lisette's were.

"Who is Leroy? What band member was removed? What does all of this have to do with Troy Turner's murder?" Mrs. Applebaum was exasperated.

Lisette ignored her. "Troy talked to the director of *Last Laugh* before getting on that yacht. So he would have been paying close attention to that band, unlike most viewers, who would just see them as the background filler they're meant to be. He must have recognized Leroy later on at dinner. At some point, he probably cornered him, got him to reveal why that saxophone player was removed from filming."

"Excuse me, I'm still here, you know? I want answers. What in heaven's name does a saxophone player have to do with anything? Don't tell me I'll have to see that silly film again to learn the truth."

"Mrs. Applebaum, I'm afraid I'll have to cut our meeting short." Byron rose from his chair.

"What?" Now it was Mrs. Applebaum's turn to be appalled.

"Nonsense, Byron. This can wait. We don't even know where Leroy is right now."

"Fortunately, you have a private detective on hand who can help you find out."

"Now see here, I'm a paying client!"

"Actually, you haven't paid yet, and I haven't agreed to take your case."

Mrs. Applebaum instantly opened her purse and pulled out her checkbook. "I'll pay right now, extra if you tell me who really shot Troy Turner and why."

Goodness, she was as bad as Hedley and Lorlene. "I don't know yet."

"You're lying!"

Lisette coughed out an incredulous laugh.

"Thank you for your time, Mrs. Applebaum," Byron said, coming around to place a hand on the small of Lisette's back. "Roberta, if you would please see Mrs. Applebaum out, reschedule for another time."

"If you think I'm going to work with you after—hey, where do you think you're going? How dare you! Wait, I'll double the pay. Just tell me, *tell me!*"

"Goodness, I'd forgotten how rabid people get about Hollywood news," Lisette said as Byron quickly ushered her out of the office.

"I'll have hell to pay for that, but it's worth it. I want to be there to see what our friend, Mr. Johnson has to say for himself."

"How are we going to find him? I'm certain the Satin Club isn't open right now, and even if it was, there's no assurance he'll be there. It's the middle of the week."

"This is Hollywood, anything is possible."

"Is it true what Mrs. Applebaum said, that Verity has been released on bail?"

"I imagine, with the new information given by Lennie, her attorney has asked for another bail hearing. Heck, they may have even dropped the charges."

"Surely not!"

"It's Byron, not Shirley, Darling."

It took a moment for Lisette to realize what he said. Instead of admonishing him about taking the case seriously, she laughed. Perhaps it was being on the cusp of solving this bothersome murder that allowed a little levity to ease her sensibilities.

"You can call me Bob if we solve this case, Shirley."

Byron laughed as he opened the car door for her, as he had led her to his car instead of hers. She thought about insisting on taking her car, then dismissed it. If she was going to shed a bit of that ambitious, no-nonsense Lisette, allowing him to chauffeur her was harmless, enjoyable even.

Besides, she had no idea where they were going.

Byron seemed to read her thoughts and turned to her with a grin. "I have an inkling where our friend Mr. Johnson might be. It was something he said when we were talking to him."

Lisette wracked her brain trying to remember what it was that could have given away what he did for a day job. The options were oddly as limited as they were limitless. It was hard enough for a white man to get a job these days which left them, and especially everyone else, doing whatever odd job they could get their hands on. She recalled they had discussed Verity, then the proof that was "on the ship the whole time"—Lisette was still disgruntled about that sly little reference to himself—then he had bid them adieu before—

"'Salutations and good night'—or rather good day. You think he works for the Good Day Fruit & Produce Company?"

"One of California's biggest employers. They had a warehouse about a block from my station up in San Francisco. I'd see that darn slogan painted on the sign at the entrance every time I passed it. Me and the boys in the department, we'd jokingly greet each other with it in the morning. Otherwise, how often do you see grown men saying 'salutations, and good day.'"

"A lot of people say 'salutations', and maybe add 'good day.'"

"Again, when is the last time you heard a grown man say it...other than someone who works for or near that company? Enough to have it etched onto their brain."

"Well...I mean..." Lisette realized she hadn't, not unless they were poking fun at the company's slogan as Byron had said. She, of course, knew Good Day Fruit & Produce, as her family had worked with them to distribute and sell their oranges. Every representative they'd met from that company had greeted them with a cheerful, "Salutations and good day!" It got to the point where Harlan and she, even her father on occasion, would also mockingly repeat it to one another.

"I'm ashamed I didn't catch the reference myself. Perhaps I heard it too much growing up. You're right though, I don't see someone like Leroy saying it, unless he's heard it enough to use it himself, even if mockingly."

"All part of good detective work, Bob."

"Gee, thanks, I'll have to remember that, Shirley."

They both laughed again.

The Good Day Fruit & Produce warehouse was understandably located by the water. They had their own shipping line as well. It was no wonder they were one of the largest employers. The entrance was manned by a guard, and neither of them could think of an excuse to get past him. Lisette didn't want to place any unnecessary attention on Leroy by claiming they were there to see him. Fortunately, it was nearing five o'clock, when most men took off for the day. Since Lisette hadn't eaten lunch, they picked up some sandwiches and Coca-Cola to-go and ate in the car while they waited for Leroy to leave for the day.

"My uncle wanted to act, or at least be around actresses. He and I used to perform these colorful acts and jokes, just to get my grandmother's heart rate going. But he'd always been her favorite. Still, he made family gatherings bearable even if my mother and Uncle Jacob tended to become exasperated by him. Of course, that seance was the last time..." Lisette trailed off, remembering how that horrible night had ended.

Byron seamlessly drew her attention to more enjoyable fare. "But you are close with the rest of your family, your parents and brother?"

She smiled. "Yes, Herbie gives me two weeks off for Christmas, and I go home every holiday. Harlan seems to have taken on all of my recklessness after the fact. I became the responsible child and he turned into a dare-devil with his love of car racing. My mother continuously frets over him, when I used to be the one causing her to have heart palpitations."

"I think there's still a bit of that girl in you. We'll work on it."

Lisette laughed. "In heaven's name, why?"

"Because you obviously miss her."

"She was nothing but trouble."

"All part of good detective work, Bob."

She laughed again. "And what about your family? Tell me more about your older sister."

"She's great. Looked out for me as a kid. I was scrawny and only shot up to my current height late in life. That made me an easy target. She once punched a boy for bullying me."

"No!" Lisette gasped, but she was awfully impressed.

"Yes, indeed. My mother is also the proper sort. Fretted that she'd never grow into a lady. Blessedly, that prophecy has turned out to be true. Mia is no lady." He laughed. "I can't wait for you to meet her."

Lisette grinned. "Is that an invitation?"

"Sure, Darling," he said without hesitation.

"Shouldn't you take me on a proper date first—one you haven't bartered for?"

"Okay, Darling. Once we solve this case, I'm officially taking you out."

"That isn't asking me, that's a demand."

"I already know you'll say yes."

"Do you?"

"Oh yes."

Lisette bit back a smile, but before she could respond, her eye was caught by the first of the men leaving for the day. "Look."

Byron turned to stare at the front entrance as well. They both studied the men who exited. The large mass of bodies was a surprising mix of all races. Most of them were laborers, dressed in overalls or other work clothes. They carried about them that mix of weariness from a hard day's physical work and relief that they were finally done for the day.

"There he is!" Lisette exclaimed when she noted him.

There had been the possibility that Byron's assumption might have been wrong.

They both exited the car and walked over to confront him. Leroy was wearing overalls, covered in dust and grime. No doubt men like him were given the worst of the jobs. There was still a sheen of sweat that glistened on his dark skin. He pulled off his cap and wiped some of it away with the back of his hand before putting it on again. That's when he noticed Lisette and Byron approaching. His eyes narrowed with suspicion.

"Well, it seems you found me," he said with resignation. "I don't know what more you expect from me."

"Tell me about the saxophone player, the one in *Last Laugh*."

His gaze solidified, penetrating Lisette for a long moment. "Well, well, well, someone's been sniffing around."

"Did you know him? Why did Verity want him off the movie?"

He seemed to be mulling something over in his head, then he finally sighed. He gestured, waving them to cross the street with him for a bit of privacy. "Y'all are going to make me miss my bus."

"I'll drive you where you need to go. Just tell us everything you know," Byron said.

Leroy exhaled a humorless laugh and shook his head. "That movie...we all thought it was the beginning of making it big, dumb as we were. Then Maurice, he saw that Verity gal."

"Or as you knew her then, Marie LeBlanc," Lisette said, her voice filled with accusation.

Leroy just smiled. "Yeah, I knew her as such back then. I didn't think nothin' of it until I got on that yacht. You see,

Maurice got to thinking he recognized her from his home back in Baton Rouge. The way she was eyeing him, she knew him too, most definitely not as a friend. The next day, he was gone."

"Did he tell you how he knew her? What it was he knew about her that had him gone?"

"No, he was well paid and well out of town by then. We weren't all that close to begin with. Just two fellas picked to play an instrument in a film. I figured there had been the kind of history between the two of them that she didn't want to get out." He gave them a meaningful look. "By then, that little girl had Lennie wrapped around her finger, and then some."

"So when did you figure it out? You said it was on the yacht. Last time we spoke, you said it was there the whole time. I assume you were referring to yourself?"

"I guess you could say I *was* referring to myself," Leroy said with an enigmatic smile. "But that ain't the sum total of it."

Lisette stared at him in frustration. He was being cryptic again, and she was this close to blowing her wig if it meant getting a direct answer.

"Think about it," he said, sounding like a teacher leading along a student who is close to getting an answer. "It was pretty much everywhere you looked on that boat."

Now, Lisette felt she needed to figure it out on her own if it was that obvious. Everywhere on that boat?

She gasped. "Black and white!"

The smile on Leroy's face—and that of Byron, who had apparently figured it out before her—confirmed what she was now certain of.

"Crackers! She really was taunting us all, wasn't she?" Lisette said, her voice filled with awe at Verity's boldness.

"The theme of the party, the masks, even those darn drinks with just a sprinkling of black seeds on top. Verity is mixed race."

"Which officially means she's colored, especially where she comes from," Leroy said.

"But...she looks just like me!" Lisette thought back to when she and Troy had been dancing. The way he pulled up her mask and pawed at her face. Now, she saw it all in a new light, his look of wonder as he stared at her.

Leroy laughed. "You'd be surprised, Miss Darling. I've seen folks such as myself come out as white as the fallen snow. I don't blame her for trying to pass. I've seen it done too many times to count. There's a code we kin abide by, we don't tell. Times are hard for everyone, why ruin it for someone trying to get ahead?"

"I suppose I was just another prop in her little masquerade."

"As was I. Though, I don't think she was quite expecting me. She probably didn't even remember me from that film. Unfortunately for her, Mr. Turner did."

"Troy had been paying close attention to that particular scene. It's no wonder he would have later recognized you when you came to play during dinner."

"Yeah, he cornered me well and good, right after that screening. He applied a bit more pressure than you two did to get at the truth." Leroy's lips thinned with anger. "I told him as much as I knew. I guess he guessed the rest quickly enough."

"Faster than I did." Lisette was still annoyed it had taken her so long. Perhaps it was Verity's gall that had thwarted her. Something she was willing to kill over being dangled so dangerously in front of everyone's faces.

Why?

Perhaps it was as Patricia had claimed, Verity saw the word "no" as a challenge. Or perhaps she was just testing how far her "passing" would go, especially when compared to her doppelgänger, who wasn't passing.

"Even the name she chose down in Louisiana was a nice little taunt. LeBlanc? White?" Lisette said, shaking her head in wonder.

Leroy chuckled. "I have to admire the girl. She's got chutzpah, as they say it back in New York. Annabelle Damon, that's what Maurice said the girl he knew was named. That's about all I got out of him before he was gone."

"Joann said Troy was a mean drunk and Geoff proclaimed him a bigot. He must have said all the wrong things to her, in the most insulting way, including her real name. I can imagine she saw everything she had worked for crumbling before her eyes, and the insult was just the spark she needed to commit murder." Lisette coughed out a sardonic laugh. "She'd been bold enough with the party. Why not be just as bold with the shooting? My goodness, I too almost admire the girl!"

"I don't blame you," Leroy said, pulling out a pack of cigarettes to smoke one.

"I assume you kept most of this from the police?" Byron said in a wry tone.

Leroy snorted as he struck a match and lit his cigarette. He sucked in a puff, then let it out. "I know better than to get involved in a case this messy. Let them wade through the muck. I get dirty enough in my day job."

"Bethany was murdered, Leroy."

"And I'm guessing it was because that girl got too big for her britches as well," he retorted. "She always struck me as an ambitious one, wanting more than what's given. She must have applied the pressure to the wrong person."

"Do you think it was Lennie who killed her?" Byron asked.

He shrugged as he took another draw on his cigarette. "I know that man had a soft spot for Verity, Marie...Annabelle, whatever you want to call her. He'd protect her from a murder charge, but kill for her?" He shrugged again, uncertain.

"I suppose there's only one way to find out," Byron said. "Go straight to the source and ask him ourselves. This time, armed with new information."

CHAPTER TWENTY-EIGHT

BYRON DROVE LEROY HOME, then he and Lisette continued to Lennie's home in Beverly Hills. He'd posted his bail and was home again. The press camped outside the front gate made Lisette wonder why he hadn't simply escaped to a private hotel. Then, she remembered the murder case was the hottest thing in the press currently. There'd be nowhere he could escape that they wouldn't find him. At least at home, he could provide the private security that was presently barricading the press from storming his front door.

Lisette and Byron pushed their way through to get to one of the guards. Enough of the press recognized her to know she was tied to the case, and they were already perking their ears in anticipation. She knew mentioning anything glaringly related to the case, especially with regard to motive, would only have the press going into attack mode. Instead, she had written down exactly one word on a piece of folded paper and slipped it to the guard.

"This is an urgent message for Lennie Lamar. It's critical that he get it now. Could you please deliver it? Tell him

Lisette Darling and her friend would like to speak with him. Or we could simply go to the police."

He stared at her, assessing whether this was some ploy.

"We won't try to get past you by force," she assured him. "I suspect he'll invite us in once he reads what's on that note."

He unfolded it and read, either to satisfy his own curiosity or to make sure it wasn't a threat. His brow wrinkled in puzzlement, and his eyes flashed back up to Lisette, filled with suspicion. Still, the note was innocuous enough, along with the not-so-subtle threat about the police, to have him taking it inside. The other guard, moved closer to Byron and Lisette, now regarding them with more interest.

Immediately the questions from the press began.

"What was on the note?"

"Is it tied to the Troy Turner Murder? The Bethany Ford murder?"

"You mentioned the police, what is their connection?"

Lisette ignored them all, waiting for the guard to come back. It took almost half a minute before he did.

If anything, he had an even deeper look of suspicion on his face as he came back. "You and only you, and your friend, may enter. Anyone else will be trespassing."

Naturally, that did nothing to stop the surge of press trying to get in.

"Now, now, folks, you heard what I just said!" the guard yelled. "Do you really want to be carted off by the police? You think storming Mr. Lamar's property will get you what you're looking for? Stand back!"

Lennie waited until they were at the door before he opened it and quickly ushered them in. They heard the sound of the cameras trying to get a good shot, even as fast as they were to enter. He wordlessly led them into his den toward the back of the house. The drapes were of course closed. It wouldn't have been beyond the press to gain access to a perfect shot from a neighbor's home. Both Lisette and Byron came to a stop when they saw who was already seated in the den.

"Verity," Lisette breathed out. No wonder there was so much press outside.

She stared back with dull animosity in her eyes. "Why not call me by my real name?"

"Which name? You've changed it enough," Lisette retorted, feeling her vigor return. She boldly walked in and sat across from Verity. Byron took the other chair. Lennie remained standing next to the armrest of the couch on which Verity was seated, looking like her bodyguard.

"The one you so carelessly wrote on that slip of paper." Verity's mouth hitched up on one side. "I had them all fooled."

"Yes, even me, I confess. Is that why you invited me on that trip? To show just how—"

"White I am? Is that the word you want?" Now her smile was even more sardonic. "Yes, I wanted to see just how far I could go. Would anyone figure it out?"

Lennie grimaced, as though he had warned her prior to her little stunt. Perhaps that's what they had been fighting about the night Troy was murdered.

"It would have worked...if not for that stupid jazz band. That's what I get for leaving it up to Patti and Betts." She frowned, her nostrils flaring in anger. "Out of all the jazz bands in the city.... Heaven knows between them, they've been to them all. That trumpet player ruined everything. I suppose he was also the one to tell you my real name. Maurice was supposed to keep his mouth shut. You paid him enough," Verity said, looking up at Lennie.

"It was bound to come out eventually, Verity. That's why I warned you. Stay away from movies. You could have been happy with Franklin. He was in love with you."

"I didn't want to be some little plaything or his pathetic wifey. I wanted to make it big, to prove to everyone, all those horrible people back home that..." A tear ran down her cheek. Lennie gently placed a hand on her shoulder.

"But...murder?" Lisette said, not unsympathetically.

"Troy deserved it. The awful things he said. The threats he made. I don't regret it one bit." She coughed out a harsh laugh. "It almost worked, me getting away with it. Even after all that, Franklin was completely under my spell. He had everyone saying up was down, right was left....black was white." She grinned, but there was little humor in it.

"But Bethany got greedy," Byron hinted.

Verity coughed out another laugh. "She did. She was never satisfied with anything. I should have known better. As long as I had more than her, she wanted that. Franklin would have given her almost anything she wanted...all for me." A proud look came to her face, undercurrents of smugness turning it into a gloat. "But she knew better than anyone that information is power."

"Did she learn the truth?" Lisette asked in surprise.

"Of course not."

There was something in the way she said it that made Lisette think otherwise. Though, she couldn't figure out how Bethany might have found out.

"And she had ammunition against you, literally," Lisette said. "She was the one to take the gun off the boat, wasn't she?"

Verity smiled. "Franklin was smart about his little hiding places. He liked the idea that we shared a secret passage to each other while on board. I took advantage of it.

After he'd sent everyone to their rooms, I left Patti and Betts, claiming I needed to go to the lady's room. It was easy enough to get past the skipper guarding the room. He was the only one standing guard and I simply sneaked in from another hallway. I picked up the gun right from where I had dropped it. But there were too many of the crew beyond that, wandering around outside. I couldn't risk being seen throwing it overboard. So, I had to detour back to my room. The hiding place was in the small closet. I was worried the police would do another, more thorough search once the trial date got closer, so I had Betts take it from the boat. Obviously, I couldn't. Patti was too much of a rabbit. I figured Betts was already bought and paid for, so why not trust her with this?"

"So, she didn't really come to threaten you with it, did she Lennie?" Lisette asked.

He remained ambiguously silent.

"You're still willing to go to prison for Bethany's murder?" Lisette was incredulous.

"He won't. That gun practically cements a case of self-defense," Verity insisted.

"And conveniently takes the heat off you as a suspect in Troy's murder."

Verity stared back with a defiant gaze. "I'm a survivor, Lisette. You wouldn't begin to understand what I've gone through to get where I am."

"You don't know anything about me."

She gave Lisette a sardonic look. "I know at least one thing."

She wasn't sure if Verity was talking about her race or the history of murder in her family. She didn't really care.

"Bethany deserves better than that legacy, no matter

what she did while alive. There's a way to get justice, and it isn't by killing someone, or framing them for murder."

Lennie's hand slipped from Verity's shoulder. Lisette eyed him, noting the guilty look on his face. Actually, it wasn't so much guilt as it was conflict.

"You have to be honest about everything, Lennie. I don't see you as a murderer, and I think even you have regrets about blaming Bethany for Troy's murder, no matter how convenient it is after the fact. Verity's secret is out, or soon will be. There's no reason to protect her anymore."

"Shut up," Verity practically snarled. "You don't know what you're talking about."

"You don't," Lennie said, so quietly Lisette almost didn't hear him. He wore a sad expression and turned away when Lisette tried to make eye contact.

She realized she was missing something. "If it wasn't self-defense, why kill her Lennie?"

He blinked, a troubled look on his face.

"Why move her body to West Hollywood from Beverly Hills?" Byron asked, studying him closely.

That question seemed to spark a note of alarm in him.

"Was it to create a jurisdictional mess? Just as what happened in Troy's murder?" Lisette followed up with. The small smirk that came to Verity's face made Lisette wonder if that had been planned as well. "Was that your doing? Keeping the yacht going back and forth between international waters?"

"No," she admitted, her smirk disappearing. "That was Franklin. We had a bit of gambling planned for later on. Fine for international waters. But he wanted us in California waters while he talked with Geoff, just in case any business was done." She frowned with irritation, but that also disappeared underneath a devilish smile. "But it worked out nicely, what with the locals and the feds battling it out as far as who took over the case."

"Is that where you got the idea, Lennie?" Byron asked, still focused on him.

He looked so defeated and torn, Lisette almost felt sorry for him. He wasn't like Verity, defiant in the face of murder. Killing Bethany, even for the sake of someone he cared about, would have had him riddled with guilt.

"Who are you protecting?" Byron prodded.

"Mama bear," Lisette whispered as it hit her. "It was Cynthia Bethany went to, or more likely Neville, who then told her. But Cynthia was the mama grizzly bear who would do anything to protect her family."

The instant reaction from both Lennie and Verity confirmed it for her.

"She didn't—"

Lennie placed a hand on Verity's shoulder, silencing her protest of denial. "It's over, Verity. We have to tell the truth now."

"Is that how Bethany discovered the truth about you? From Cynthia? Because Neville is...your father?"

Verity blinked in surprise. "Not at all. Neville is..." She looked off to the side, blinking back a sudden onset of tears. "He's the only one who ever looked out for me back home. He's my brother...half-brother, anyway."

So that was it.

"His bastard of a father—" Verity coughed out a laugh. "Though who am I to call anyone a bastard? That man took advantage of my mother. She was young, cleaned their house, took care of their kids. Then, when she became...*inconvenient*, he threw her out with the trash. It was particularly problematic when I came out looking the way I did."

She was still looking off to the side as she continued, the Louisiana slipping back into her voice. "You know in that state, all it takes on tiny trace to make you anything but white? One little drop, like a few sprinkles of poppy seeds."

She turned back to face Lisette and Byron. "Neville was old enough to know what had happened. He hated his father for that. To the point he changed his own last name. He took sympathy on us, gave Mama a bit of money when he could. Even when he moved away—he always wanted to work in the entertainment business—he sent money to us.

"Still, I hated it, the way people looked at us, treated us. At times I even hated her for bringin' me into this world. I couldn't wait to get away. I'd seen people do it—*my* people. They simply walked off, never to be seen again. We all knew, but no one talked about it. They just let 'em slip away to start their new lives, passin' as white. And why not me? So, one day I left that little town just outside of Baton Rouge and hopped on a train as Marie LeBlanc. It's funny how different they treat you when they think you're one thing and not the other. It was such an easy mask to slip on. Life became so...effortless. As though there was nothin' I couldn't do. That's why I picked the swan for my mask, transformed from the ugly duckling. That story always struck me as a child, it was the inspiration for everything I became."

Verity's eyes glazed as though remembering it all. "Neville was surprised to see me when I arrived on his doorstep, but not nearly as surprised as his wife." Her mouth twisted with contempt as she gave a harsh laugh. "She knew the whole story, of course. Wanted nothin' to do with me, the bastard daughter. But Neville saw me as kin, so he helped me. I had to pretend I was old enough to be on my own, of course. Cynthia wasn't about to let me into their home. I was fine with that. Heaven knows I'd learned to get what I wanted on my own in life by then. Becoming Marie LeBlanc had made me bold...perhaps even reckless.

"*Last Laugh* was the first time that mask threatened to fall off. Ain't that the most ironic name in retrospect? Maurice knew who I was, and I recognized him, sure enough. I wanted him gone before he could talk to anyone, let it slip. So I..." She glanced at Lennie and then looked away, the first bit of self-reproach touching her expression.

"It's fine. I know you were using me," Lennie said, his hand back on her shoulder. "I suppose I felt sorry for you. When I paid him off, he told me the truth. That's when I knew I had to protect you. I suppose I empathized with your struggle."

Verity smiled and patted the hand on her shoulder.

"So Bethany went to Cynthia and...she was the one to...?"

Verity looked at Lisette and nodded. "Bethany had the gun. She knew that Neville and I went back a ways, all the way back to Louisiana. Like you, she thought he was my father. She wanted to know everything, thought there was some information she could use to get more out of Franklin. Cynthia was offended by the suggestion it was Neville who'd fathered me. If only she'd kept her dang mouth shut. How could she be so...so...*stupid!*"

"She panicked is all," Lennie continued. "Hitting Bethany with the vase was purely out of panic. She was pressuring her at gunpoint, after all. Cynthia called me, knowing how much I cared about Verity. She was the one to suggest framing Bethany for the murder and claim self-defense. Not for herself, of course, she just didn't want her family affected. I'm under no such constraints so..."

231

Lisette felt her admiration for him kick in. Lennie had such a soft heart, it could have gotten him into trouble.

"Franklin...did you tell him the truth?" Lisette asked, mostly out of curiosity.

The bitterness that touched Verity's features said as much. "He wanted to know why I shot Troy, the real reason. Said he would protect me either way, but he wanted the truth. My recklessness kicked in. I suppose I wanted to see if it would matter to him." She arched a brow. "Apparently, it did."

That explained Geoff's suggestion Franklin had been embarrassed when he spoke with him the morning after.

"The good news was, he now had even more reason to keep everyone silent." She breathed out a bitter laugh. "I doubt I'll ever see that man again, but he'll keep my secret all the same."

"Were you planning on framing me?" Lisette had to ask; the final nagging question.

Verity's mouth pursed just a bit and she gave an offhanded shrug. "How could I not? You'd conveniently left, right after fighting with him. I'd only invited you when I noticed how similar we looked to one another. It was the icing on the cake. Suggesting it had been you who shot him, not me, was the final bit of armor I had to protect myself. Enough to create reasonable doubt, at any rate. People are awfully sympathetic toward pretty women, particularly if they are of a certain *persuasion*."

She didn't seem apologetic, and Lisette wasn't inclined to be sore about it. No need to ask Verity to humble herself anymore in life, a life which had been decidedly more difficult than Lisette's had been.

"No need to worry your pretty little head. I'm turning myself in." Verity met Byron and then Lisette with a level gaze laced with a strong current of defiance. "I won't tell them any of what I just confessed, the truth about why I shot Troy Turner."

She was silently asking them to do the same. Lisette looked at Byron, who arched a brow back at her. Between them, they silently agreed.

"So long as you do turn yourself in," Lisette said. "We have no reason to reveal anything we've learned. After all, it would only be hearsay."

Verity relaxed with a small nod. "I suspect when Cynthia also has to, she'll keep our little secret." She breathed out a soft, cynical laugh. "Well, you've got what you came for. I'm going to have Lennie take me in. He's taken care of me this whole time," Verity said, turning to give him a grateful smile.

The mask dropped for just a moment, all the daring and boldness gone, and Lisette saw the real Verity—or rather, Annabelle Damon, that she had once been. It made Lisette think of the armor and mask she too had carried after she'd come to California around the same age as Verity had.

Perhaps it was time for Lisette to shed hers as well.

EPILOGUE

That Friday evening, Lisette was putting away the day's papers which she had re-read throughout the day. Cynthia Frost had finally turned herself in as Verity Vance already had. The feds had ceded jurisdiction to the locals, washing their hands of the murder. There had been no mention of the real reason for either Troy Turner's or Bethany Ford's death.

Verity claimed Troy had made lewd comments and improper advances toward her, to the point she worried about her safety. While it wasn't quite a clear-cut case of self-defense, the prosecutor had sympathized enough to lower the charges to manslaughter. Verity had been right, not knowing the truth about her, public sentiment was decidedly in her favor. Maybe even Joann's suggestion might prove true: she'd eventually be the biggest star Hollywood had seen yet.

If Verity was smart, she'd leave Hollywood far behind once she got out of prison.

Cynthia's claim was that Bethany had come to her, brandishing the gun and demanding money. She had panicked and hit her with the vase. Moving the body from Beverly Hills to West Hollywood had been done solely to draw attention away from herself and her family. Lisette was less pleased with that cover, but the truth would have been the sort of cheap dirt the media would feed on for weeks. Lisette wasn't about to ruin the lives of Neville and their boys, who were all innocent, by airing the sordid reality. In a way, it was close enough to the truth. If Bethany hadn't gotten greedy—in her case for information rather than money—she'd still be alive. Neville was taking a break from producing films to look after his family.

As for the others aboard that yacht the prior weekend, there were already rumors about how well others had made out in the aftermath. Hedley's contract with Winthorpe Media had supposedly been renewed for another five years, and with quite the increase in pay.

The other scuttlebutt was that Joann Golden was in talks with three major publishers, each of them vying for the chance to publish her biographical tell-all (but presumably not *entirely* tell-all).

The owner of the yacht had been in seclusion with absolutely no word to the press for the past week. Lisette could only imagine the strong talking-to Edgar had given Franklin all the way from New York.

With no garishly public trial, the press would lose interest by the next week and move on to the next Hollywood scandal. Lisette had already moved on.

In fact, she was rather looking forward to that evening.

As though on cue, there was a knock on the door to her office before Byron simply opened it and walked in. He was picking her up from work—saving her a trip home on the bus—and then taking her on a proper date. They were going to dinner and a movie (anything but a comedy), then for a night of jazz at a certain slightly seedy club they both knew of.

"How's tricks, Bob?" Byron said with that boyish grin she adored so much.

"They're jumpin', Shirley," she quipped right back in a zany voice. "Let me just pop in to say bye to Herbie."

Byron followed her into her boss's office.

"So you've come to whisk my lovely assistant away for the evening, have you?" Herbie said with a grin. "Good. She deserves a fun night on the town. Just behave yourself, young man."

"I have no intention of doing any such thing, good sir," Byron said with mock offense.

"Nor do I," Lisette scoffed.

Herbie laughed. "Before you trot off for the evening, this came for you, my dear." He reached into his top drawer and pulled out a bright red envelope. "I saved it so you have something to be giddy over during the weekend."

Lisette's brow wrinkled with curiosity as she accepted the envelope. It was the size of a greeting card. When she saw the return address, she realized it was an invitation.

"Rutherford Heart?" Lisette exclaimed, eagerly opening the envelope. The tell-tale gold paper peeking from inside told her what she wanted to know. "He's invited me to his holiday party!"

"*The* Rutherford Heart?" Byron said, craning his neck to get a look at the invitation elegantly printed on thick, gold paper.

"Up at his Castle by the Coast," Lisette said, a grin on her face as she read the details. "It's one of the most exclusive parties in the country. Everyone wants to see what's inside that behemoth he's taken twenty years to finish building."

Lisette looked up at Herbie. "Are you sure this was for me, not you? He only invites people he thinks are interesting."

"Apparently he finds you meet that qualification. As you can see, it's your name that is quite clearly printed on the outside."

"It must have to do with this case. He and Franklin have always been at odds. I'm to be nothing more than a cheap gossip."

"No one says you have to be. No one says you even have to go. That would be something, saying no to Rutherford?" Herbie laughed just thinking of the insult.

"You've been invited once. What was it like?"

"Oh, that fellow just wanted a bit of tawdry dirt I was privy to as well. I suspect you'll handle it with as much aplomb as I did, Lisette—giving him absolutely nothing. The best Christmas present I had that year was watching him steam with frustration."

"I'm going. I'm too curious not to."

"I agree it's worth it. Say what you will about the man and his eccentric nature, but he has built quite possibly the most beautiful yet ostentatious residence I've ever set my eyes on. And I've seen the inside of most of the mansions in this city."

"Well, I suppose we have something to celebrate tonight," Byron said.

"All the more so since it says I can bring a guest. You have any plans just before the holidays, Mr. Linley? What do you say to a bit of mischief and mistletoe at a swanky little party?"

Byron grinned back at Lisette. "I say...it's a date, Miss Darling."

AUTHOR'S NOTE

Why yes, this book is very much borrowed from the speculation and rumor surrounding a fateful party aboard William Randolph Hearst's yacht in 1924. While the circumstances surrounding the death of the film producer Thomas H. Ince remain a matter of debate and conspiracy theory, the events that have taken place in *Murder Without Motive* are very much fiction and not based on what may have happened in real life, speculative or otherwise.

LOCH NESS

The story of Loch Ness having babies was taken straight from an article in the *New York Times*: **Monster of Loch Ness Now Raising a Family**. A few pupils from a boys' school claimed they had seen it—do with that what you will. Perhaps Lucy had a point about trusting the news. The article is dated Sunday, June 27, 1937—yes I took liberties with the date, but that's the beauty of being a fictional author. It was too much fun not to include.

MICROFILM

As a former librarian, I'm fascinated (and sometimes horrified) by the stories related to archiving and preserving information. I've worked at the University of Houston Law Library, which was completely underwater after one hurricane. It has since been used in library & information science classes as a lesson in protecting, repairing, and rebuilding collections.

While microform has been patented since the 19th century, commercial usage of it to preserve information didn't really start until the 1920s. In 1935 the Recordak division of Kodak expanded and began recording and archiving the New York Times. Three years later Harvard University Library began its Foreign Newspaper Project, and University Microfilms, Inc. was founded to microfilm doctoral dissertations.

BEVERLY HILLS

Sadly, this part of the book was also taken from real life. In my research of Los Angeles, I naturally wanted to include Beverly Hills, as many stars made the city their home. The first subdivision was built in 1907 as a planned community complete with white-only restrictive covenants preventing the sale of a home to anyone else, including Jewish people. It was in the 1940s that court cases were brought to enforce these covenants, with a certain notable actor offering his support. So as not to ruin your day, I'll allow you to google the name. Never meet your heroes, as they say, even when they are dead.

LOUISIANA LAW

This was a fascinating bit of research and when I read about it, I thought it would be interesting to include. Yes, in the State of Louisiana, a person was legally defined as "colored" on their birth certificate if they had a "trace" of black blood. In 1970, it became more defined as having more than 1/32 black ancestry. This lasted well into the 1980s when, in 1983, a woman named Susie Guillory Phipps, discovered she wasn't white only after getting a copy of her birth certificate. The authorities had to trace her ancestry back 223 years—her great-great-great-great-grandmother—to certify that, according to state law, she wasn't white, as she'd always assumed.

GET YOUR FREE BOOK!

Mischief at The Peacock Club

**A bold theft at the infamous Peacock Club.
Can Penelope solve it to save her own neck?**

1924 New York
Penelope "Pen" Banks has spent the past two years making
ends meet by playing cards. It's another Saturday night at
The Peacock Club, one of her favorite haunts, and she has

243

her sights set on a big fish, who just happens to be the special guest of the infamous Jack Sweeney.

After inducing Rupert Cartland, into a game of cards, Pen thinks it just might be her lucky night. Unfortunately, before the night ends, Rupert has been robbed—his diamond cuff links, ruby pinky ring, gold watch, and wallet...all gone!

With The Peacock Club's reputation on the line, Mr. Sweeney, aided by the heavy hand of his chief underling Tommy Callahan, is holding everyone captive until the culprit is found.

For the promise of a nice payoff, not to mention escaping the club in one piece, Penelope Banks is willing to put her unique mind to work to find out just who stole the goods.

This is a prequel novella to the *Penelope Banks Murder Mysteries* series, taking place at The Peacock Club before Penelope Banks became a private investigator.

Access your book at the link below:
https://dl.bookfunnel.com/4sv9fir4h3

Made in the USA
Las Vegas, NV
21 October 2024

10188796R00138